THE BRITTLE RIDDLE

A short story based on true events

Jack Anderson

- Squadron Books -

THE BRITTLE RIDDLE

First published by Squadron Books - Anderson IP / LLC

The Brittle Riddle – Copyright © 2023 by Jack Anderson in collaboration with Squadron Books

Printed in the United States of America

All rights reserved. No part of this publication may be reproduced, stored, or transmitted in any form or by any means, electronic, mechanical, photocopying, recording, scanning, or otherwise without written permission from the publisher. It is illegal to copy this book, post it to a website, or distribute it by any other means without permission.

First addition 2024

Squadron Books is a registered trademark of Anderson IP LLC

Cover art by: Nick Anderson and squadronposters.com

Edited by: Carol Sampson

CONTENTS:

INTRODUCTION	1
PROLOGUE (DRAGONS)	3
1 FAMILY	11
2 BRAVERY	15
3 PORTRAITS	19
4 MOON SHADOW / AMERICAN PIE	23
5 TRUST	27
6 THE PARTY	35
7 BLUEPRINT	37
8 HELP IN TIME	41
9 FRIENDSHIP	45
10 SCIENCE	49
11 CLUE	53
12 FOUND SOMETHING	57
13 ANOTHER DIRECTION	63
14 PATIENCE	67
15 SINS OF THE FATHER (WITCHES)	73
16 TRUTH AND JUSTICE	81
17 HOME	85
EPILOGUE	89

- FOR NANCY -

INTRODUCTION:

"THE BRITTLE RIDDLE" BY - JACK ANDERSON

I have witnessed many strange and unexplainable events throughout my life. No other event has touched me more deeply as in 1972, when the glass covered portrait photo of my sister Nancy crashed to the ground at my feet, at the exact moment she was brutally murdered over 3000 miles away. This event has led my family and I on a 50-year journey to try and resolve what would eventually become one of the nation's oldest and most difficult cold case mysteries ever solved.

This is the true story of our mysterious *Brittle Riddle*...

Portrait photo of Nancy Anderson

God bless all who tame dragons.

PROLOGUE (DRAGONS)

2 years after the attack on Pearl Harbor ***Hawaii*** on December 7th, 1941, our dad joined the Navy when he reached the minimum age. After completing basic training, he learned the specific trade of a *"Boilerman"* which came with the responsibility of keeping a ship's engines powered. Once trained, he was assigned to a supply ship in the Pacific theater of WWII, the USS Cygnus (AF 23). His ship provided material for missions such as the landings in Guadalcanal by the 1st Marine Division.

During that same time, our mother worked at a Chevrolet auto parts plant that was converted to support the war effort. Our dad eventually referred to himself as a devout *"Chevy man"* as that was the brand of car we always owned. However, we knew it was more likely because of his love for our mom.

While on leave, our dad married our mom who waited anxiously for him to return safely. Eventually he was honorably discharged after the war ended. The trade of "Boilerman" became very valuable as he was quickly employed by a factory in a neighboring town. This job paid well, affording our parents the ability to support a large family in their quaint small Michigan town of Bay City.

Big families like ours put the sonic *"Boom!"* in the post-World War II Baby boom generation - a birth group defined as people born from 1946 to 1964 and often described as a *"shockwave"* of population growth like no other in modern history. Our parents would eventually procreate a family 3 times larger than most families of the time, which averaged 3.5 children per household in the 1960s.

In January of 1959 after the fetal growth hormone instructions built into my **DNA** completed its task, I was born. I arrived on a frozen winter day into this amazing family that would eventually include **10 children**. We lived happily together in a nice home that our father proudly built and were lucky to have wonderful parents who loved us immensely. - Collectively, we are **"The Andersons"**.

As a child, one of the first homework assignments I received in elementary school was to describe our family. Therefore, I interviewed our dad and he said, *"I really wanted **2** children"*. When I questioned our mom, she said, *"I really wanted 5 children"*. The next day at school, I gave my report and stated these facts and concluded at the end:

*"**2** times 5 equals 10 and that's what they got!"*

To me, the multiplication factor made perfect sense and was the practical reasoning for our family's size. (It also didn't hurt to slip in some math for extra credit).

We typically had snow for the holiday season, however, during the Christmas of 1965 there was none. Our dad could see how clearly disappointed we were because without snow, *"how was Santa going to land his sleigh with our presents?"* So, he gathered all 10 of us into the family room on Christmas Eve and said, *"If all of you pray hard enough, maybe it will snow!"* (And so, we did). We awoke Christmas morning to a massive snowstorm. After realizing what just happened, our dad said: *"Next time, only half of you pray!"*

We all laughed and were amazed at the true power of prayer.

In addition to teaching us right from wrong, our dad made sure we understood how to respect and value people over possessions. He also took each child out on their birthday for ice cream, even though he was diabetic and couldn't take pleasure in the tasty treat. He did these things, and much more, spending some special time with each one of us. That's the person he was, a good man of faith and family.

In the 1960s our father worked swing shift at the factory, rotating weekly between days, afternoons, and midnights. However, he would also occasionally pick up extra shifts if called...

Our dad was critically injured in an industrial accident on one of those extra shifts in the bitter cold winter of 1966. It was exactly **2** weeks after that snowstorm, on shift **#2**, just **2** hours after reporting to work, and **2** minutes after his coffee break when a boiler exploded, burning him severely. Even though he was fatally injured, with 3rd degree burns over 90% of his body, he reached the control shut-off panel to save part of the factory and the lives of many of his coworkers.

Every so often there are moments in life where the love between a father and son is immeasurable and delivering a message of truth without saying any words can be profound.

Our eldest brother Mike (#1) was attending school at a seminary in a nearby town at the time of our dad's accident. He was immediately summoned to the hospital and only told that his father was injured with no details provided. Once Mike arrived, he was escorted to the door of our dad's room and hurriedly ushered in while expecting to see something like possibly a broken arm...

As Mike entered the room, he did not recognize the person lying in the bed in front of him. Facing our severely injured dad for the 1st time, Mike was shocked. Seeing the look on his son's face, our dad simply said, "Mike, is it that bad"? The doctors had yet to tell our dad how terrible it really was. The gut-wrenching reality of seeing his dad brutally burned and revealing to him the truth simply by the look on his horrified and puzzled face is a message no 18-year-old should have to experience or deliver.

We all stayed home from school that first week after the accident. By the second week our mom decided it was time to restore some type of normal and therefore we went back to school. Once I arrived in my 1st grade Catholic school class, my teacher (a kindly nun), came to my desk in the front row and said *"Jack, gather all your things and follow me."* (And so, I did). I slowly trailed behind her with my arms overflowing with all earthly possessions in what felt like a humiliating walk of shame.

The Andersons always held the privilege of sitting in the front of class via alphabetical order, however that day I was sentenced to reside in the *"Bad Boy"* section. Once seated next to Tommy *"Zimmerman"*, I was dreadfully aware of being strategically relocated closer to the **door** while feeling gut-punched that things must not be going well for dad.

That following week the entire class heard the soft knock at the door. I could clearly see my aunt and uncle along with my little sister Jan (#9) peeking through the side window next to the door. Our teacher slowly walked over and opened it. She looked at them, and then they all turned to look back at me, all the while never saying a single word. I instinctively stood up and reluctantly fell in line behind my sister.

The four of us marched out the front entranceway single file and trudged across the cold, slushy, dirty, snow-covered parking lot. My sister and I quietly entered the back seat of their car and we all drove away in deafening silence. After a short while, Jan broke through the calm frigid air and said, *"where're we goin'?"* My aunt turned around and gave us the most beautiful heartwarming smile while struggling to breathe out any resemblance of recognizable sounds. - I spared her the trouble and simply said *"Daddy's dead"*.

We continued our journey home in complete silence except for some muffled sobbing emanating from the back seat. The lack of a counter reply confirmed our fears. - Every so often there are moments in life where the love between a brother and sister is immeasurable and delivering a message of truth by saying the fewest words possible. Our dad died **2** weeks and **2** days after that horrific accident and is now eternally a *hero*.

When we arrived home, our house was filled with every neighbor, friend, and extended family member from miles around. The grieving was intense, and I found myself screaming at God for taking our dad. Most families had only a few kids and some other dads were not as good as ours, so why didn't He take one of them instead? There are *ten of us* and we *NEED HIM*! – I believe the lesson we learned at school that day was *"life can be cruel"*.

The accident was the result of an unknown design flaw built into the massive boiler system back in the 1920's before he was even born. Somehow it seems like after **2** decades of peace the war found our dad and *took him* from us. Heat is your friend to keep the cold at bay, except when a boiler blows up at work killing your dad.

We buried him a few days after my 7th birthday on another terribly cold winter day. Our entire village attended the solemn parade to central park where rows of stones neatly aligned, a ceremony was held, speeches were made, and our mother reluctantly received the prestigious flag of the national kingdom (a consolation prize I suppose).

Whenever we drove past that old factory our hearts would sink as we gazed upon the towering smokestacks clawing ominously at the sky. We knew there were men like our dad at the bottom of each stack, fighting a dragon, struggling to tame the beast to support *their* families.

The constant billowing of smoke releasing into the atmosphere always gave the impression it was skywriting taunting messages like *"We took your dad"* or *"Surrender Andersons"*! As it cast its gloomy shadow across the face of the horizon and combined with a nauseating odor emitting from the dragon's breath, it overwhelmed the senses.

It seems to me that when you work as a heroic knight in shining armor to slay fire breathing dragons, no matter what shield or sword is used, *sometimes the dragons win*. Our family was left to muster forced acceptance at the conclusion of this epic battle. We didn't know what the future held as we understood the unfortunate truth that it wouldn't be easy without him powering our ship. Without the steam *he* provided, I feared we may drift aimlessly on the vast ocean of life. The loss of our dad was devastating, and I wished we prayed for *him* instead of snow on Christmas Eve.

(Maybe that would have saved him).

My fears were justified, however, we still had the love of each other, the comfort of a good home, and we tried to make the best of everything.

With the passing of our dad, our mom became the center of our universe and she refused to be thought of as a damsel in distress (even though she clearly was). She found herself raising us alone for many years, navigating each day utilizing her internal compass and faith in God. That year her children ranged in ages from 1 to 18.

We were a full representation of youth: infant, preschool, grade school, middle school, high school, and college. As a widow, our mother worked long hours tending to her large family. However, the older siblings would often step up and help care for the younger ones as needed. (I can never thank them enough!)

Still, it was not easy. Our mom was kind, quiet, and strong in her determination to move forward. Her smile and laughter lit up every room, but it was her gentle compassion toward others, including strangers, that set her apart.

She continued teaching us right from wrong and what was truly important in life. We were taught to share everything, and selfishness was never tolerated. That's the person she was, a good woman of faith and family. After losing our dad, all we could do was try and carry on without losing hope or faith in what really matters...
With the exception of our dad, **we still have each other**!

1 FAMILY

The Anderson Family (1962).

In addition to our dad (Merle, aka "Andy") and mom (Thelma), our first names are: (clockwise in photo) Mike, Carol, Gail, Nancy, Mary, Betty, Jim, Jack, Janet, and Bill (not yet born). However, we also have our informal *"number"*. Mike is #1, Carol #2, and so on…

My name is *Jack* and I'm #8 of 10 (sitting on our mom's lap).

It's not only our name, position on the family tree, and personalities that make us different from one another, it's also the very nature of our cells. Like everyone, we each received 50% of our biological information from our dad and 50% from our mom. However, the content mixture of this information is not *exactly* the same. It's the unique genetic proportional shades of ancestral data we each received that makes us slightly distinct looking, yet relative to each other.

When it came to personalities, our sister **Nancy (#4)** had an adventurous imagination and a particular talent for acting and directing. One day when Nancy was about 9 years old, while at school, she just decided it was her birthday. (It was not). She invited all her friends to our house that afternoon for her birthday party. When Nancy arrived home and told our mother, our mom was shocked!

Our amazing super-mom played along and quickly went into action. She drove to the store and purchased hotdogs, cake, and ice cream. The party was a success and went much as Nancy anticipated.
The performance she created was enjoyed by all (except our mother who did most of the work). Our remarkable mom reprimanded Nancy, however, she compassionately did not punish her. None the less, our mom did hold back all birthday gifts Nancy received until her *real* birthday, six months later.

When Nancy was a sophomore in high school, she rode the bus with Gail (#3) who was a Junior. Gail soon learned that Nancy possessed some unique, quirky, and creative abilities.

Our mother was very conservative and did not allow any of my sisters to wear mini-skirts or make-up to school. So, every morning Nancy and Gail would say goodbye to mom and set off for the bus in their traditional clothes. Once on the bus (to Gail's surprise) Nancy would pull out a needle and thread and proceed to hem her skirt shorter, turning her outfit into a 1960's fashion trendy mini skirt. When she finished, she would then artistically put on make-up and arrive at school looking like a different person.

Gail never said anything to Nancy and was simply confused as to why anyone would go through all that trouble just to spend the day at school. On the way home, Nancy reversed the entire process by taking the hem out of her skirt and removing the make-up. Nancy did this every school day, while Gail watched the laborious transformation in amazement. To Nancy, it was simply a way to be relevant as a teenager.

Gail never betrayed Nancy's trust in the alteration by mentioning anything to our mother, even though she was always baffled by the entire theatrical route. She was, however, astonished by Nancy's confidence, courage, and conviction to act in a sort of non-confrontational (yet rebellious) way. It was a personality trait that Gail admired and previously never knew Nancy was capable of. Gail learned to appreciate the determination and inner strength that Nancy seemed to master in performing any role she chose.

Nancy also had the ability to quickly memorize all the lines of any movie. Our favorite family movie growing up was the 1939 classic **"The Wizard of Oz"** which became a traditional television special broadcast annual event starting in 1959 (the year I was born).

Nancy saw our large family as a casting opportunity, so she would produce live in-home productions and make sure everyone *had a part to play*. The younger brothers were always recruited (more like drafted) into playing the militant part of the *"Lollipop Guild"*. Nancy, of course, would act the part of *Dorothy*. She could sing the song *"Somewhere Over the Rainbow"* better than most. She could also perform every part, word for word, and would make sure we all rehearsed our lines to perfection.

Growing up in a large family of 10 kids was challenging, fun, and at times just a little crazy - especially when we had additional people over like friends or extended family. We would often sing songs, dance (with Nancy typically leading the endeavor), and play all sorts of games.   To visitors, we may have seemed like *Munchkins* simply living every day together in our colorful world. I treasure those family memories we had together even more as the years pass.

This story is based on some of those memories and the true events surrounding the mysterious murder of our beloved *Nancy*.

2 BRAVERY

Glass is an inorganic solid material that is usually transparent or *translucent* as well as hard, brittle, and **impervious** to the natural elements. It's the **"brittle"** part that can get you into trouble.

One day in the winter of 1970 we had another crowd of people over at our house. It was yet again a brutal and bitter cold Michigan winter that year. I was eleven years old and remember it like it was yesterday. That day my sister Nancy had her friend Marty over. The **2** of them were good friends, the best of friends. They were inseparable and did everything together. It was their senior year in High School and graduation was just around the corner in the warmer days.

That evening they both walked outside our back patio **door** for just a moment to check on something. In doing so, they left the door *"open"*. Me, in my ever state of trying to keep warm, walked by and thought *"Why is this door open, its freezing outside?"* So, I shut it... It was the practical thing to do! Unfortunately for Marty, my mom did an extremely thorough job of cleaning that large glass door earlier in the day resulting in a very translucent (and *"brittle"*) natural element.

As Marty re-entered our house through what looked to be the still unshut, opened **door**, it shattered into many small, sharp, and not so kind objects. The sound of the *shattering glass* was alarming and upon impact it cut her severely. Nancy *courageously* made sure Marty made it to the emergency room where she received many stitches. Nancy also gave a *heartfelt* apology to Marty and her family. I felt horrible as we were left to clean up the **shards of glass and blood that lay at our feet**. (Being practical is sometimes overrated).

There are those who believe the spiritual meaning of *broken glass* signifies that you are about to go through a significant change in your life or a warning about a relationship that you hold dear. I'm not sure about these things, however if true, I may be guilty of setting off an unintended chain of events.

Around that same time our eldest brother, Mike (#1), was attending college in Colorado. Our mom visited him and fell in love with the mountains and the sunshine and when she returned home to Michigan, she had a renewed spark of life in her eyes. We soon learned that we were all moving to Colorado after the school year ended. Many generations of Andersons lived in our small Michigan town and now change was in our future. My mom was the bravest person I would ever know. Moving all of us to a new unknown land was no simple task.

Early that summer Marty and Nancy graduated from High School. Marty decided to join the Air Force and so did Nancy. However, at the last moment Nancy determined the military was not for her. The Vietnam War was still raging, and it detoured her from joining in on this adventure with her best friend. So, Nancy, like the rest of us, made the move to Colorado.

Once we arrived in our new town of Arvada, Colorado, we all agreed that mom was right. The scenery was breathtaking, and the mountains and sunshine were truly amazing (and no dragons to contend with). We soon found ourselves busy unpacking and preparing for the new school year and meeting new friends. We attended a new church and embraced this *brave* world we found ourselves living in. **Change *can* be Good.**

Nancy worked a few jobs in Colorado, but she kept thinking about the military adventure she avoided and the friend she missed. Nancy and Marty wrote to each other often, keeping informed as to what life brought their way. At one point, Nancy randomly visited a fortune teller at the State Fair who told her *"You're not long for this world"* and *"your life will be cut short, you will not live beyond your teenage years."* Nancy just laughed.

In the *Wizard of Oz*, Dorothy also meets a travelling fortune teller (Professor Marvel), who immediately suspects that she is running away from home. Using *sleight of hand*, he secretly inserts a *family portrait photo* of Dorothy and her aunt into a *glass crystal ball* for an illusional effect. He then pretends to reveal her future with the intent of reuniting Dorothy with her aunt and says, *"You're Auntie Em has fallen ill from worry over you"*.

I will admit that our mother also had many moments of *worry* over Nancy as well. She too found it difficult to restrain her free and bold spirit, especially after Nancy turned 18. After leaving Michigan, it seemed as if Nancy could not connect with any new friends in Colorado as deeply as she did with her childhood friends who were all moving forward in life. This left her with a wandering spirit for adventure and a desire to see more of the world, even if for just a moment in time.

Eventually, Nancy decided she wanted her own adventure - one that involved standing on her own **2** feet, with peace, tranquility, sunshine, and no Vietnam. Like Dorothy states in The Wizard of Oz *"Someplace where there isn't any trouble"*. She knew just the place... **Hawaii**.

Our dad visited Hawaii during his military service in the Pacific during WWII and occasionally he talked about it. Nancy imagined it was *a land that she heard of once in a lullaby*, as it sounded like the place of *dreams*. Hawaii is the only U.S. tropical state, and it attracts tourists from around the world with its warm climate, scenery, and amazing beaches. It's also known as the *"Rainbow State"*.

For Nancy, Hawaii was her *Somewhere over the Rainbow*.

On October 21st, 1971, **2** weeks before her 19th birthday, Nancy courageously moved to the islands. Before leaving, our mother gave Nancy $**2**,000.00 to help her with the move which was Nancy's portion of the insurance money from when our father died. On October **22**nd she rented an apartment, pre-paying $**2**00.00 in advance. She soon obtained a job and set a budget.

Nancy understood that she was no longer a child and was determined to take responsibility for her 19-year-old life while also experiencing a new adventure in paradise. It seemed as if *dreams that you dare to dream really do come true...*

Life is Good

Waikiki beach **(1972)**   **Our dad 1944**

3 PORTRAITS

On December 23rd, after spending **2** months and **2** days in Hawaii, Nancy returned home to Colorado for Christmas vacation. She arrived all smiles, tan, and bearing some gifts. The biggest gift, however, was simply having everyone home together again. It was fun and we had fresh Colorado snow (without even praying for it) which added to the Christmas decorations.

I received a new *Cat Stevens* record from Nancy and the haunting lyrics of the new hit song *"Moon Shadow"* soon became my favorite.

>*"Oh, I'm bein' followed by a moonshadow,*
>
>*Yes I'm bein' followed by a moonshadow.*
>
>*And if I ever lose my legs, I won't moan, and I won't beg,*
>
>*Yes if I ever lose my legs… I won't have to walk no more.*
>
>*Did it take long to find me? I asked the faithful light.*
>
>**I'm bein' followed by a moonshadow…"**

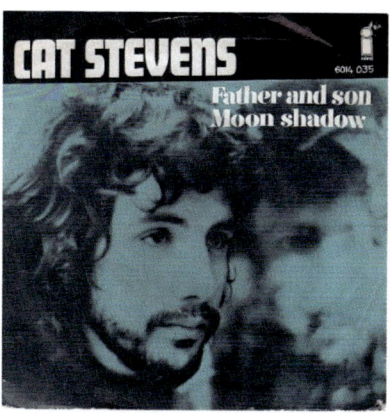

Nancy was excited to be home and could not go to sleep easily on her first night back. She shared a room with Mary (#5) and they both stayed awake very late talking about everything. Nancy said she would return to Hawaii after the holidays and save enough money to eventually move back to the Denver area.

It was Mary's senior year in high school and Nancy wanted the **2** of them to be roommates in their own apartment and attend College in Denver together that fall. Nancy knew Hawaii was a temporary experience so this would be yet another new adventure for them both. She now held bigger long-term dreams and understood a higher education could help make them a reality. Hawaii was great; however, it was somehow *starting to sour*.

As Mary drifted off to sleep, Nancy said: *"Mary, if anything ever happens to me, remember this name ____.* When Nancy realized Mary may have dozed off, she repeated: "Mary, are you awake? This is important! **If anything happens to me, remember this name ____.**"

To this day Mary cannot recall the specific name. However, she remembers it was a unique **2**-syllable ethnic sounding male name (something like: **" - *dro*"**).

We were still not completely moved into our new home in Colorado, so Nancy decided to give yet another gift to the family. She created a wall mural in our basement using the most recent school photos (and the graduation photo of herself and the older siblings) as well as the most current portrait photos available for our mom and dad. Nancy refused help from others as she wanted this special creation to be an exclusive Christmas gift from her to all of us.

If she could, she would have used *sleight of hand* to secretly insert each photo into their *glass* covered photo frames. However, that wasn't possible under the watchful eyes of our large family. So, she proceeded openly on her own without a cast or crew. This was Nancy's way of producing and directing yet another (although independent) theatrical performance, while showing her love for the entire family through this unique art project.

Each of these 12 photos were hung with precision, care, and kindness, in our proper (yet artistic) natural family order: Dad, Mom, Mike, Carol, Gail, Nancy, Mary, Betty, Jim, Jack, Janet, and Bill. This would be the last gift we would receive from Nancy before she returned to Hawaii.

The result was a graphic snapshot in time of *"The Andersons"*.

Wall mural of family portraits in our basement (1971-72)

Nancys photo 2nd row from left - top.

After Christmas vacation ended Nancy was hesitant to return to Hawaii. At one point she said, *"I don't want to go back."* However, all her personal belongings were still there so it was the practical thing to do. After New Year's Day Nancy returned to Hawaii on January **2**nd, 1972…

In the following days things were getting back to normal as the Holiday Season came to an end. On January 7th my brothers (Jim #7 and Bill #10) and I were playing a game of pool with some of our friends down in our basement. There was a particular shot that required tilting the back end of the pool stick ever so slightly higher to avoid bumping the wall. It was my friend's turn and unfortunately for him, he did not make this maneuver correctly. We all heard the faint *"thump"* as the stick hit the wall (near my photo / bottom right). - **And then it fell…**

Our mom was facing the television (and not us) while sewing something by hand when the alarming sound of the *shattering glass* startled everyone. Immediately our mom screamed one word *"Nancy!"* without even looking in our direction. We all felt an unsettling rush, like an overwhelming sensation of - *something touching us deep inside*.

The photo that fell seemed to *"jump"* off the wall as it didn't even touch any other photos below it. I looked down at my feet and saw the shattered glass covering the face of my sister's portrait. *It was Nancy's!* Of the 12 photos *she* hung, only *hers* fell to the ground and *how did our mother know it was Nancy's?* I thought **that's strange.** I felt horrible and started to clean up the broken glass that lay at my feet. **We would soon learn the gravity of this event!**

4 MOON SHADOW / AMERICAN PIE

It was a beautiful Saturday morning the next day, January 8th, 1972. Snow still covered the ground, but the Colorado sun was starting to shine and melt the cold away. It was the 6th anniversary of our dad's fatal accident.

Late that afternoon our mom drove us to Saturday evening church. On our return home we stopped for ice cream in honor of our dad while witnessing the most breathtaking and peaceful sunset along the foothills of the Rocky Mountains. We listened for the 1st time to an amazing new song on the radio called *"American Pie"* by Don McLean:

"A long, long time ago, I can still remember
How that music used to make me smile
And I knew if I had my chance
That I could make those people dance
And maybe they'd be happy for a while.

But February made me shiver
With every paper I'd deliver
Bad news on the doorstep
I couldn't take one more step
I can't remember if I cried
When I read about his widowed bride
But something touched me deep inside
The day the music died.

So, bye, bye, Miss American Pie
Drove my Chevy to The Levee, but The Levee was dry
And them good old boys were drinkin' whiskey in Rye
Singin', "This'll be the day that I die
This'll be the day that I die".

Every so often there are moments in life where the love between a mother and son is immeasurable and delivering a message of unfortunate truth cannot possibly contain the appropriate words.

When we returned home, our brother Mike (#1) was waiting for us at our doorstep. He had the dreadful responsibility of once again informing a parent of unimaginable news. Pulling our mother aside, he revealed the most horrific message a mother should never hear, and no 24-year-old should ever have to deliver. Her daughter (our sister) Nancy was brutally *murdered* in Hawaii the previous day.

Our family was hit by this horrific *tornado* of tragedy and our *Dorothy* was carried away.

That evening our family was devastated and incapsulated in grief once again. No one could sleep… It was not only the horrific loss of our sister and the anniversary of our dad's fatal accident, but it was also the way in which Nancy was killed and the dreadful fear that it may happen again. Her vicious murder was much like a terrorist attack. Not knowing if it was going to continue its rampage against others in the family was unsettling. That night we all huddled into our mom's room and shared in the pain of constant, restless anguish.

Adding to all this was the strange *foreboding* issue of her portrait photo crashing to the floor the day before. From what we can piece together, **she was killed at the exact moment her photo (which she hung up), shattered on the ground.** She was brutally stabbed 63 times in her apartment. I will admit that to this day, I don't go to bed without *closing all the curtains* and locking *all the doors*.

**Paradise is peaceful and tranquil,
except when someone kills your sister.**

Nancy Anderson's graduation portrait photo and a card she carried with her.

The name of the lead crime scene detective working on her murder case was **"Detective Moon"**. The song **"Moon Shadow"** will never mean the same and the song **"American Pie"** has a strange new significance.

Like *glass*, life is fragile and can't always be put back together. Nancy was left there to die with no trip to the emergency room and no apologies. She was found soon after being killed and no one knew who did this. Somehow it seems that *Vietnam* had found Nancy, the *hourglass shattered*, and the *Wicked Witch killed our Dorothy*.

Her body was flown back to Michigan and buried next to our dad, on yet another bitter cold winter day. After her funeral service, we all stood in silence and grief with their graves at our feet. Love can be measured in joy. Unfortunately, it can more accurately be measured in the depth of pain. We have no words other than... **Who did this?**

That day I secretly swore to God that I would find whoever did this and made a promise to Nancy that I would never stop until we found justice for her. (I was certain everyone else felt the same.) There seemed to be a new slow burning fire that was now permanently etched into me to **DO SOMETHING!**

Marty was also there. However, she had to quickly return to her new duty station as the military only recognizes family members, not friends, for bereavement leave. As she flew away, she looked outside her window to see if she could find Nancy's face in the clouds and the *shadows of the moon...*

We lost contact with Marty and would not meet again for many years.

The reasoning for the 24-hour delay in notifying our family seems to stem from the Honolulu Police believing Nancy moved to Hawaii directly from Bay City, Michigan and not from Arvada, Colorado. They ended up contacting a local newspaper in Bay City which led them to our sister (#2) Carol's husband Mark, who was back in Michigan.   He returned to work there soon after the Christmas holiday concluded. Mark relayed the horrific news to our brother (#1) Mike in Colorado, who was home at the time. This resulted in Mike notifying the family instead of the local Arvada police as was customary.

Either way it was once again *bad news on our doorstep, and we couldn't take one more step, after something touched us deep inside... the day our* **Nancy died***...*

5 TRUST

That day Nancy was very visible, spending most of her time taking care of financial obligations. She walked the local area, picked up her paycheck at work, deposited money at her bank (Bank of Hawaii, Waikiki Branch #**2**), paid bills with money orders, and scheduled appointments. She *was* busy being responsible. She typically worked the day shift at a local restaurant, however on Friday, January 7th, 1972, she may possibly have taken the **2**nd shift that evening.

Nancy, as well as most of her friends and coworkers, did not own cars during that time. Everyone typically walked or took mass transit as everything they needed was within a small distance near Waikiki beach. One of the many questions we have is: *Did Nancy seek a ride to work or somewhere else that afternoon*?

She was killed on a sunny afternoon around 4:30 Hawaii time. Her roommate was at home in the next bedroom, and she didn't hear anything. The police determined that the walls were soundproof, and her apartment **door** was more than likely locked. It also required a key code to get into her apartment building (or you had to be *buzzed-in* by the occupant). Her apartment at **2222** *Aloha Drive* was on the 7th floor of a 10-story *castle tower-like* building. Each floor had 4 apartment units. This did not seem to be a random act of an opportunistic serial killer, as there was nothing convenient about reaching Nancy.

This led the police to believe that Nancy may have let someone in. (to get a ride somewhere?).

Nancy's apartment building entrance key code system

2222 Aloha Drive

In Hawaiian the word *"Aloha"* is used as a greeting for both hello and *goodbye*. However, it also means Love, Peace, and Compassion.

One of the first things the police told our family was ***"it must have been someone who Nancy trusted"***. Nancy had a genetic trait like our mother's (yet less guarded). Her smile and laughter lit up every room, however it was her gentle compassion toward others, including strangers, that set her apart. Nancy's overly trusting nature may have been deadly.

She was not raped or robbed, and by the many wounds on her forearms (regarded as defensive wounds) she more than likely tried in vain to defend herself.

One strange event that occurred was a visit by **2 door-to-door** salesmen for an appointment previously arranged earlier in the day. The salesmen arrived at Nancy's apartment at 3:00 that afternoon, right before she had to get ready for work. These salesmen sold many Westinghouse items, including **knives**. In doing so, she received a free gift and a chance to win over **$2**,000.00 in prizes. (For Nancy, it was the practical thing to do). Eventually the salesmen were vetted and cleared by the police.

Sales ticket with appointment time.

Everyone that the police could determine Nancy knew on the island was required to take a lie detector test (and later in time a DNA test). All Nancy's friends and coworkers in Hawaii were cleared by the police based on the currently available information. Her case went cold.

There is not a day that goes by that we don't think of our sister Nancy and how much she means to us. Whenever we get together as a family, the conversation soon drifts to Nancy and the strange events surrounding her murder. We are diligent and determined to find the truth about what happened that day.

We don't know how long our *journey for justice* will take. No matter the distance, we will *follow the road* to wherever it leads and pursue the justice we seek. **We will *pull back any curtains* we find covering our way, looking for the answers.** We are not pursuing vengeance, rather the simple truth. *What happened that day and* **who killed our sister?**

After Nancy's murder it was apparent to us that there was more in life to avoid than *wild animals in the woods*. We clearly knew that real *dragons* and *witches* do exist, so caution prevailed as we didn't know who the killer was, where he dwelt, or if he (or she) would strike again.

Not knowing can be dreadful. Ever since I was 12 years old, after Nancy was killed, I found that most people don't want to hear about uncomfortable subjects like *murder* (and that's understandable). So, I learned not to talk about it to anyone but family or close friends. If the topic ever did arise with people I'd recently met, I would often hear things like *"let it go"*, as if I just found a small scratch on a new car.

Being stabbed 63 times is well over once per second, or more accurately, being stabbed for several minutes – It sickened me and just added to my anguish and determination to never let it go!

In the 1960s and 70s grief counseling was not commonly available to children who experienced traumatic events such as the loss of a loved one. We certainly spent our time in the oven of sorrow with no professional help in trying to deal with untimely and disturbing deaths. Digesting this information left us with many ominous and unsettled questions.

However, we have our faith and the blessing of many siblings to talk with whenever, and as often, as needed. Having each other to converse with about events and feelings became invaluable as we *trust* each other. Therapy can come in many forms, and I admit that maybe in some small way, writing this story is also helping me to heal with my own personal internal struggle in trying to make sense of the senseless. (It's the practical thing to do).

It seems to me when our *Dorothy arrived in Oz, her house did not land on and kill the witch's sister. However, somehow the witch killed our sister.* Fate is a tricky result of circumstances in time.

As a family, we calculated hundreds of scenarios through the imagination of our minds on what may have possibly happened when Nancy was murdered and by whom. I can honestly say that it's almost as important to know **who did not** murder our sister as **who did**.

Over time anyone who ever knew Nancy became a suspect to us, as we eventually ran everyone through the private gauntlet of probabilities in our thoughts (including people we cared about). This was not because we obtained any new relevant information, but rather the issue of our sister's murder was worthy of all considerations and our desire to know was immense.

The absence of information left only speculation and conspiracy theories proliferated in the dark until someone with a *magic wand* of enlightenment could make the truth appear visible for all to see. Meanwhile, we had nothing solid to go by and no clear evidence other than false assumptions. It seemed that we were left with an unsolvable **"riddle"**.

At one point we were told by the police that with no eyewitnesses, murder weapon, or other evidence: *"The best we could ever hope for is that someday, someone confesses."* We never put much confidence in this possibility and knew we had little to nothing. However, if somehow any other evidence, no matter how minor, could eventually come into play, would we have *something*? If so, will it be enough?

Hope, faith, and trust can be a powerful and unstoppable force of nature and humanity of which our family has an abundance...

In 1985, Carol (**#2**) wrote a ballad (poem/song) that captures some of the mystery surrounding Nancy's life and murder. It was written to the tune of "*Greensleeves*", a traditional English folk song also known as the Christmas song of "*What Child Is This?*"

Nancy

There was a young girl, fair and sweet

who always did seek laughter.

She loved to dance, to sing, to roam;

adventure was her master.

A fortune teller told her, "Child,

you're life it is too short.

Get on with it while you have time,

the world, it is your court."

So she traveled o'er this country wide;

the country it did lead her.

The sights were many and beauty great,

though yearning did not leave her.

One trip did take her to the Isles,

there her fortune to make more.

After three weeks of life has passed,

No, after three months and more.

No fortune was there to be found;

no gold, no silver treasure.

Instead, her journey was in vain;

her heart it found no pleasure.

Strangers, many did she meet;
some friendly and some not.
Though all the strangers in the world
were friends in her way of thought.

Her picture crashed to the ground,
her mother's heart did stop.
A crack that went across her face
did pierce her mother's heart.

"*Twas only a broken glass, Mother.
It had no meaning at all."
"*Twas only a broken glass, Mother."
Her children told her – all.

The girl's heart, it was pierced through;
no more life nor journeys for her.
A stranger had been to her *door*;
a stranger with a *dagger*.

Carol (1985)

6 THE PARTY

Over the years I have witnessed and heard of many stories of spiritual connections with loved ones who have passed. Don't get me wrong, I'm not a fanatic about this topic. However, our family has experienced many strong connections with Nancy, starting when her picture portrait shattered the moment she was murdered (and even earlier when our dad was killed). We see a constant connection with both the number *"2"* (such as her Hawaii address: **2222** *Aloha Drive*) as well as **"The Wizard of Oz"**. I will cover the number **2** in a later chapter but thought I should cover at least one of the many "Oz" connections here.

In November of 1989 Betty (#6) visited Colorado Springs from the Denver area, where her sister-in-law (a high school senior at the time) was playing in a volleyball tournament. Betty decided to take her daughter and drive down to watch the game. To her surprise, Carol was also there with her twin daughters who were cheerleading. They were so happy to see each other in such an unexpected way, they sat and talked throughout the entire game.

When the game was over, Carol invited Betty back to her hotel where they were serving free hors D'oeuvres and throwing some type of party in the lobby of the hotel. Betty said, *"no thank you it's getting late, and I have a long drive ahead of me"*. Carol asked her once again convincingly in her big sister's voice. *"Betty, it will be fun!"* So, Betty changed her mind and decided to go for just a little while. When they arrived at the hotel, they were shocked to find all the waiters and waitresses dressed professionally in extremely beautiful *Wizard of Oz costumes*, as it was the theme of the party. They both enjoyed the food and each other's company, while having a great time.

After a while, Carol and Betty turned to each other and said at the same time *"Do you know what day this is? **It's Nancy's birthday!!!** She's giving herself another birthday party!"* This time however, it truly was Nancy's birthday complete with fancy food (no hotdogs), and an amazing atmosphere!

As mentioned, our favorite family movie was the *Wizard of Oz*. When it broadcast on TV each year, Nancy would insist that all of us siblings play a role while pretending we were in the movie. She always got to be *Dorothy*, while Betty (unfortunately) had to play Dorothy's dog *"Toto"*, but not this time! I think it was Nancy's way of honoring her sisters and showing love to those of us who were required to act in her plays, no matter how silly it was.

Carol and Betty were shocked and knew that only Nancy could orchestrate such a beautiful party on her birthday (or any day), and she made sure they were both invited. They felt her presence smiling down from *Somewhere over the Rainbow*, once they figured out what she had pulled off! It seemed as if Nancy had thrown herself yet another birthday party, and to me she was saying *"have a little faith, the story is not over, things will turn out fine in the end"*.

The party was a success and I'm sure it went much as Nancy anticipated. My **2** sisters raised their glasses and gave a heartfelt toast:

"We love you, Nancy, Happy Birthday!"

7 BLUEPRINT

Our dad had passed away, our mom was busy raising her children, and we were all so young when this happened to Nancy, no one was able to follow up on her murder. The years passed and eventually my brother Jim (#7) and I both joined the U.S. Navy like our father did. However, we served with the Navy *"Seabees"* (not as *"Boilermen"*). In time, I transferred over to the U.S. Air Force *"Civil Engineers"* as both organizations are military construction forces.

After my own daughter was born, I felt an urgent need to do something... anything... to move the mystery of what happened to Nancy forward. The promise I made to her years ago was haunting me (again). I knew my dad would do the same for his daughter if he could.

In November of 1994 (**22** years after Nancy was murdered) I deployed with the Oregon Air National Guard Civil Engineers to Hickam Air Force Base Hawaii. Our mission was to remodel some historic WWII buildings (which I believe our dad would have approved). Before leaving, I obtained a power of attorney from our mom so I could meet with the Honolulu Police on her behalf. The intent was to see if there was any progress and, at the very least, re-open a dialogue as over **20** years had passed. Coincidentally, I happened to be in Hawaii for Nancy's 41st Birthday.

On Monday, November 14th of that year, I met with Lieutenant Allen Napoleon who was gracious enough to give me his time. This is when we learned that there may possibly be **DNA** left at the crime scene. (And not much else could be done at that time). However, this opened the *door* for hope.

The murderer apparently cut himself in the *heartless* act of killing our sister. His blood, as well as our sister's, was found on a blue towel from Nancy's apartment that was left at the bottom of the internal stairwell. Evidently, he dropped it there before *cowardly* exiting her apartment building, turning *translucent*, and disappearing into thin air.

Nancy's apartment stairwell exited to an outside parking lot.

DNA (Deoxyribonucleic acid) is a polymer composed of **2** chains (of polynucleotide) that coil around each other to form a **double** helix. The polymer carries genetic biological instructions that make the physical part of each of us. An organism's complete set of nuclear DNA is called its genome. Organisms inherit half of their nuclear DNA from **2** different parental contributors (male and female) thus DNA also seems to reflect the number **2** in the very nature of our being.

DNA is also sometimes called the ***"blueprint of life"*** because it's the instruction manual to create, grow, function, and reproduce life on Earth. These biological instructions are now so well defined that they are specific directions to identify *one individual person* only. I came to Hawaii to work on a set of construction blueprints only to discover there was another much more important blueprint to consider (DNA).

The killer left his *construction blueprint* on Nancy's *blue towel*.

Every so often there are moments in life where the love of family is immeasurable, and the world stops with just a few spoken words. I happened to be in Hawaii again (of all places) in February of 2001 on a non-military business trip when I received a phone call that our mom had a heart attack. We all traveled from around the country to her bedside in Nevada (where she was currently living) as the surgery did not go well. We held hands while encircling her bed and prayed as she peacefully passed away.

We buried our mother next to our father and Nancy, on yet another bitter cold Michigan winter day. The loss was overwhelming once again. Our wonderful mother was the one who taught us at a young age how to move forward through tragedy and difficulties. Through example, she showed us how to get back up after life brings you to your knees and to focus on others as a remedy to resolve our own internal pain.   (The blueprint she provided for living was priceless). Whenever I asked her how she raised us alone, her reply was always *"I did not raise you all alone, God was with me!"* We learned from her how to say *goodbye* while holding onto faith that there will someday be a new *hello*.

I learned at the age of 7 that life is a temporary state of existence, not through the loss of a pet or distant relative, but through the loss of our dad. I remember looking around his new gravesite and seeing the headstones of Civil War veterans and many others who have gone before us and thinking, *someday there is an end in this life to us all.* It was a bit deep for a seven-year-old, but I knew it was true. Time is a precious treasure, and we need to guard it, as well as spend it, well. When it's my turn, I think I prefer to be laid to rest someplace warm.

8 HELP IN TIME

The realization that our mom passed away without knowing the answer to the questions *"Why did this happen? and Who did this to Nancy?"* was the stimulus my sister Carol (*#2*) needed. It motivated her to also find answers and resolve this puzzle. So, the *2* of us decided to team-up on moving Nancy's cold case forward and represent our family together.

Around this same time, Carol and her husband Mark moved from Colorado to *Nevada*. While packing, Mark unplugged an analog clock in the garage without paying any attention to the *time* on the display. After moving into their new house, he unpacked the boxes and came across this clock and noticed the hands were stopped at *2:22* and *22* seconds. He immediately showed Carol and they were both quite surprised. As mentioned, our family always associates the *#2* with Nancy.

In July of 2001 Carol wrote to Lee Donohue, Chief of Police: *"Since there is no statute of limitations on homicides, I urge you to reopen this investigation and prove to our family that all avenues of a thorough investigation have been exhausted."* Nancy's case was immediately reopened and given to Lt. Kato, a homicide detective.

In the early 2000's, as a result of our family's encouragement and request, the State of Hawaii expanded their lab to include DNA testing and also formed a Cold Case Unit devoted to unsolved murders. We beat the drum to encourage their certification into the FBI's Combined DNA Index System (CODIS) so DNA evidence could be submitted into the national CODIS software system.

Carol and I sent hundreds of emails to the many detectives who rotated into the assignment of Nancy's cold case, as well as kept the family informed of any updates. Over these past several decades we tag-teamed communicating with the cold case detectives and the family depending on who was most available at any given time. We put in countless hours trying to move Nancy's case forward.

Our family has been very fortunate to be able to meet some of the personnel involved in Nancy's case throughout the years. In addition to my visit with Lieutenant Napoleon in 1994, Carol and her husband Mark had the opportunity to be in Hawaii twice to meet with other members of the Honolulu Police Department to discuss this investigation.

In 2005 they met with Captain Arita, Detective Higa, and Lieutenant Kato. They were told by Captain Arita that he had Nancy's case and her picture on his desk, and he looked at it every day. That's the type of dedication and commitment we needed! (Yet, no new information.)

In 2017 Carol and Mark met with Detectives James Slayter and Paul Okamoto, the **2** cold case detectives working Nancy's case at the time. They were also very respectful and assured them that they were continuing to work diligently on Nancy's case. (Still, nothing new to report and we understood that the case was extremely cold.)

In 2019 I met with Detective Michael Ogawa of the Honolulu Police via Skype video conference and was asked to participate in an interview with the local Hawaii media. The police had instituted a new Crime Stoppers website and Nancy's case was the 1st to be featured. The professionalism and concern we continued to receive from the Honolulu Police was greatly appreciated by the entire family!

We need all the help we can get!

9 FRIENDSHIP

On October 11th, 2017, I received a strange text message out of the blue: "Hello. Was Nancy Anderson your sister? I'm Marty and was a good friend of hers in high school. Every once in a while, I Google her to see if there have been any new developments. I saw your name in an article tonight and that you were living in Oregon so I'm taking a guess that you are her 'little' brother. Would love to hear from you, if so. Thank you!"

I was shocked! Making contact with Nancy's best friend once again after all these years could only be a good thing. We soon started corresponding and the family received some new insight. Marty kept all the letters Nancy wrote to her. We were elated to read stories that Nancy wrote. It was like hearing from her once again!

One letter tells how Nancy felt the day before she moved to Hawaii. It reads: "... so far I'm still going, scared to death and maybe tomorrow I won't be on that plane but hope to God I have the guts! I know if I don't go I'll never forgive myself, mostly of **being afraid to live.**"

Included in these letters Nancy sent to Marty was a crossword puzzle Nancy completed, where she artfully injected her humor. It reads: *"Dear Marty when you're old and grey and looking at this remember my elephant toes and laugh! Love Nan!"*

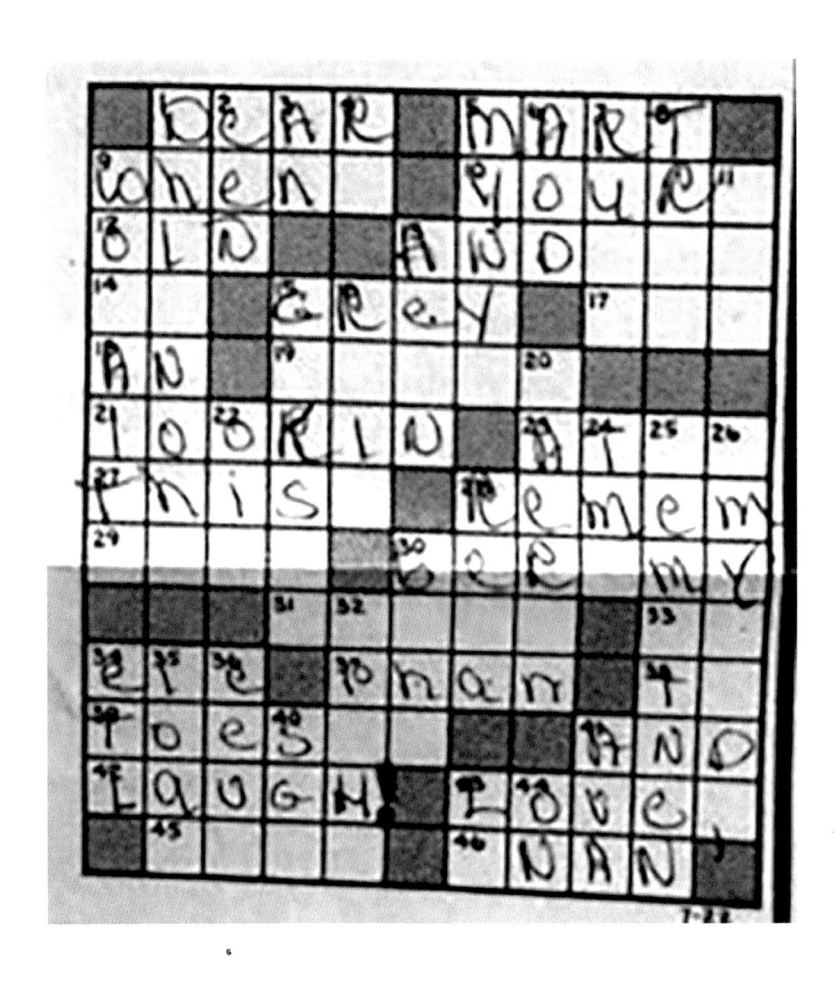

I have the same awkward genetic DNA trait with my toes, they don't move independently from each other. It's also a bit prophetic that Marty did live on in years (and Nancy did not). Another letter stated: *"When I get home, we'll both gallop off to never never land and find us a prince in shining armor. Shining! - Never dull, as they say **one's armor reflects one's personality**! See ya soon!"*

46

> When I get home, we'll both gallop off to never-never land and find us both a prince in shining armor. Shining! - Never dull, as they say one's armor reflects ones personality!
>
> See ya soon!

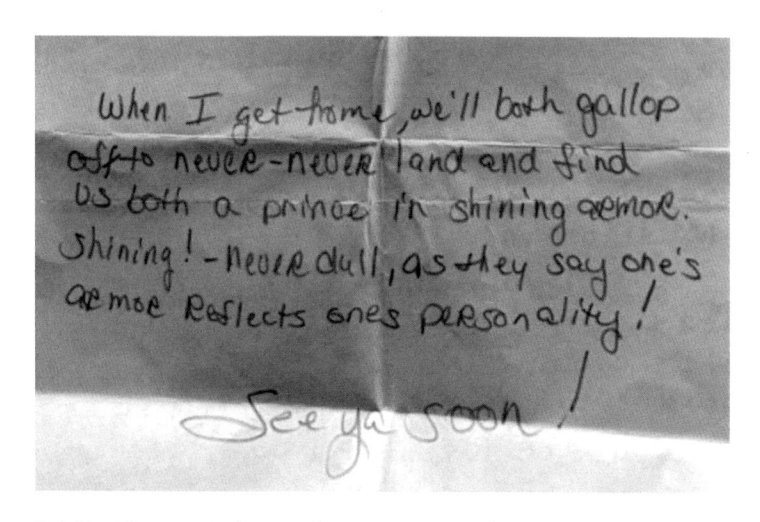

Marty did find her *Knight in Shining Armor*, has a family of her own, and is doing well. She still misses Nan.

I was the one who shut the **door** on Marty and Nancy years ago resulting in a severe injury. Marty still bears those scars to this day, and I can't help but feel guilty. However, Marty made it clear that she forgave me a long time ago as she knew it was simply an unintentional accident by a young kid. I never meant to hurt her or anyone. I just wanted to keep warm, and that open **door** was not helping my cause.

I cannot rewind time and take away the cuts both Marty and Nancy received. However, it would be good to get Nancy's murder resolved someday and honor their endearing friendship. It's comforting to know Marty has *reopened the* **door** by extending her friendship beyond Nancy, to our entire family.

We are grateful for her renewed friendship because *"a heart is not judged by how much you love; but by how much you are loved by others."*

Nancy captured her feelings about friendship in this poem.

A Simile of Friends

Friends are like the sun simply because you need them.
Your heart would freeze and never be warm,
until you've experienced friendship.

Today is the day for doing - what you haven't done.
Today is the day for spinning – the yarn you haven't spun.
Today is the day for singing – the song you haven't sung.

Tomorrow's the day you hope – will have a brighter sun.
Tomorrow's the day you hope – will bring happiness and fun.
But now's the time for undoing – all the wrong you have done.

Young for a day – then old and gray
like the rose that buds and blooms and fades and falls away.
Losing health in search of wealth
battles evading – **fate we're fighting until the curtain falls.**

Nancy (1970 - 1971)

10 SCIENCE

In 2018 we held another family reunion. As usual, the topic eventually turned to Nancy's murder. DNA technology had advanced quickly over the last several years, so we believed we might be at a point where the DNA evidence left at the crime scene could now be used in a practical way. We were hearing of DNA being applied to finding people who were adopted, missing persons, and unidentified bodies.

My brother Bill (#10) and I stayed up late one night pondering this question and the next morning we presented our hypothesis to the family. After explaining the theory, the entire family agreed it was finally possible for Nancy's extremely cold case murder to be solved through DNA! *But where do we start?*

The Anderson family reunion January 2018

Back row: Mike, Jack, Bill, Front row: Janet, Carol, Gail, Mary, and Betty - *Jim not pictured.

Unknown to us during this same time, this is exactly what was being attempted through a new science known as *genetic genealogy*. This science combines genealogy research (family trees built on historical documents) with DNA evidence used within a DNA database to find the suspect or potential relatives of the suspect. The results of this new tool are much more powerful than each discipline separately.

A few months after our family reunion, we learned that the infamous *Golden State Killer* was found utilizing this new genetic genealogy technology. We finally see a clear path forward. However, we still needed someone like a *Glinda* or a *Wizard* with a *crystal ball* to help us.

Leading this new field was, and continues to be, Genetic Genealogist *CeCe Moore*, an American genetic genealogist who has appeared as a guest on many TV shows and as a consultant on others such as *Finding Your Roots*. She has since helped law enforcement agencies in identifying suspects in over 50 cold cases in one year using DNA and genetic genealogy. In May 2020, she began appearing in a prime-time ABC television series *"The Genetic Detective"* in which each episode recounts a cold case she helped solve.

On February 5th of 2019, I reached out to CeCe Moore and simply said *"CeCe, we need your help!"*. I included a few links to recent news reports on Nancy's cold case and her Honolulu crime stoppers page. I did not expect to receive an answer. I was astonished to hear back from CeCe right away. ***"I want to help your family!"***

Our family was elated! We can never thank her enough for her gracious offer and for answering our call for help!

As far as science is concerned, I am one who believes that God created the world. In doing so, He also created the natural elements and the laws of physics (Boilers blow up under unrestricted pressure, sharp objects cut, and surgeries don't always go as planned). I can't help but presume God's laws also transcend to the spiritual world as we have witnessed the shattering of glass on the portrait of someone dearly loved when simultaneously murdered over 3,000 miles away.

Faith and science are not competing for truth, rather science is simply man's attempt to understand God's creation. Mankind and DNA are part of this creation. Science is the precise, systematic endeavor that builds and organizes knowledge in the form of testable explanations and predictions about the universe around us. DNA data is somewhat like the yearly seasonal environmental information stored in tree rings and ice cores as they all reflect consistent, repeatable, and verifiable markers of natural history.

Knowledge is power and for those of us looking for answers to murders and other violent crimes this new genetic genealogy knowledge is truly powerful. Wielded in the hands of highly skilled professionals it can seem like a *magic wand* of science. As time goes on, it's revealing more and more *witches* who have been hiding transparently in plain sight.

As humans we can choose to be a *witch* who commits vicious crimes or seek our inner *angel* of goodness by choosing good over evil (free will). Choices that affect others should have consequences. Hopefully this new science can *reveal the witch* that murdered our Nancy.

11 CLUE

To put this into perspective: The board game *"Clue"* (Hasbro, Inc.) is a popular murder-mystery game originally published in 1943 by Anthony E. Pratt. You move around the game board (a mansion) collecting clues from which to deduce which suspect murdered the game's victim (Rev. Green, Colonel Mustard, Mrs. Peacock, Professor Plum, Miss Scarlett, and Mrs. White). It's the sum-total of all the physical evidence that determines who the murderer is. It's complicated.

I am under the belief that this board game needs to be updated. It should now include any DNA evidence and a new card that can be drawn within the deck of clues. This new card just needs to have one name printed: *"CeCe"*. If you're lucky enough to draw this card when it's your turn, it's game over. Losing a family member or friend to murder is not a game. However, we felt that after almost fifty years, we just drew the CeCe card. Investigative Genetic Genealogy (IGG) can find more clues than previously thought possible.

We also requested that the Honolulu police use Parabon NanoLabs and Snapshot DNA Phenotyping Services (the best in their field). Once the administrative hurdles were cleared, they agreed. We soon found ourselves working with a new and powerful crimefighting team: The Honolulu Cold Case Detectives, Parabon NanoLabs, Snapshot DNA Phenotyping Services (which created a digital rendering of the murder suspect), and CeCe Moore. With all their help we just might get this resolved.

DNA is already starting to answer who ***did not*** murder Nancy!

Honolulu Police Department Crimestoppers / Nancy Anderson

If you have any information about this case, please contact CrimeStoppers at (808) 955-8300 (case #334785**22**).

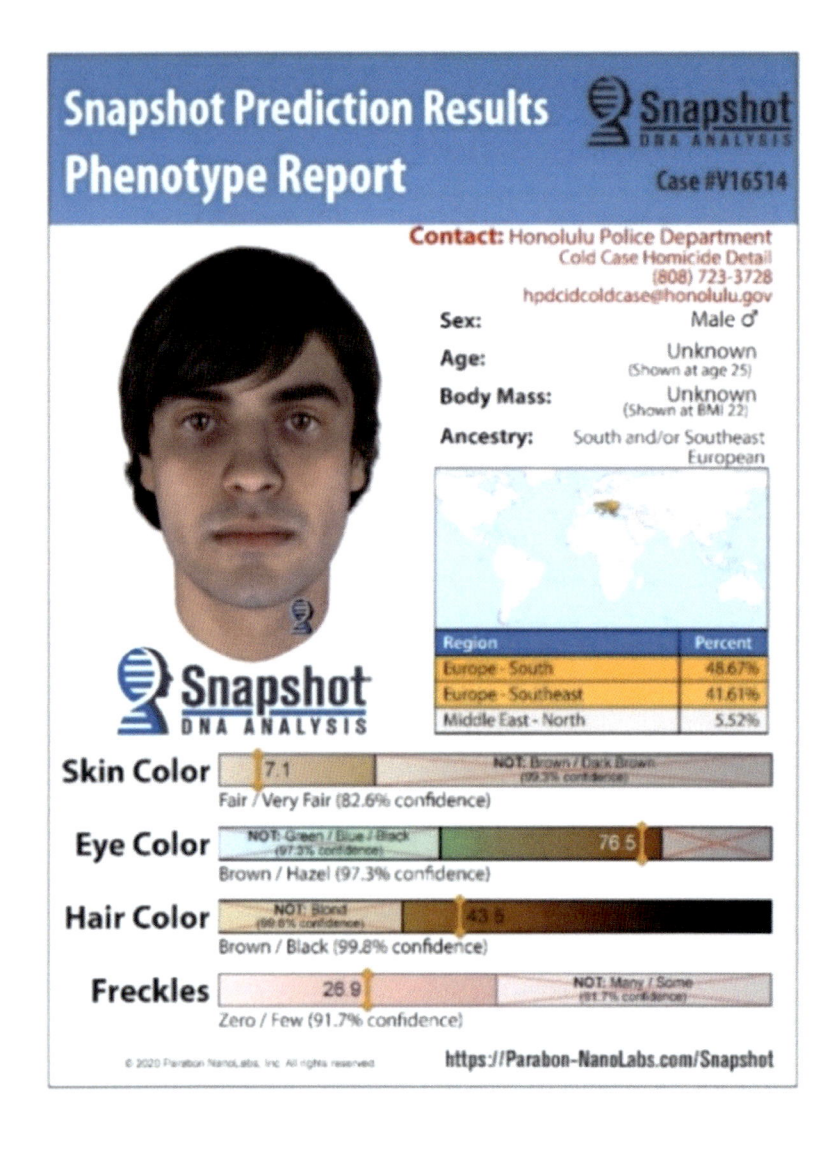

Snapshot Prediction Results — Phenotype Report
Case #V16514

Contact: Honolulu Police Department
Cold Case Homicide Detail
(808) 723-3728
hpdcidcoldcase@honolulu.gov

Sex: Male ♂
Age: Unknown (Shown at age 25)
Body Mass: Unknown (Shown at BMI 22)
Ancestry: South and/or Southeast European

Region	Percent
Europe - South	48.67%
Europe - Southeast	41.61%
Middle East - North	5.52%

Skin Color: 7.1 — Fair / Very Fair (82.6% confidence) — NOT: Brown / Dark Brown (99.3% confidence)

Eye Color: 76.5 — Brown / Hazel (97.3% confidence) — NOT: Green / Blue / Black (97.3% confidence)

Hair Color: 43.5 — Brown / Black (99.8% confidence) — NOT: Blond (99.8% confidence)

Freckles: 26.9 — Zero / Few (91.7% confidence) — NOT: Many / Some (91.7% confidence)

© 2020 Parabon NanoLabs, Inc. All rights reserved.
https://Parabon-NanoLabs.com/Snapshot

Snapshot DNA Phenotyping Services prediction results

We look forward to the new possibility of resolution.

In March of 2019, Carol and I decided to streamline our efforts to help everyone involved. Carol took the lead on communicating with the cold case detectives in Hawaii and keeping the family informed. She also became the unofficial records keeper by eventually amassing, over time, three large binders that consisted of all things Nancy. This included family documents, photos, newspaper clippings, emails, text messages, and other information.

Binders of all things about Nancy

I took the lead on communicating with CeCe Moore as well as diving into basic research into all I could find associated with cold cases involving advancements in genetic genealogy, as well as current news events related to both. This attempt was to simply try and understand what may be presently applicable and not that we could add anything new to the investigation.

In February of 2020, we learned that CeCe was conducting a workshop for DNA detectives in Nevada, not too far from where Carol and Mark lived. I was able to help coordinate a meeting and, within no time, Carol and Mark *were off to see* CeCe and they made sure to bring their binders concerning Nancy's case.

CeCe welcomed Carol and Mark like they were family. They were left with the feeling that with CeCe's help and the clues DNA can provide, it's not a matter of **IF** Nancy's case would be solved, but rather a matter of **WHEN**...

My sister Carol, CeCe Moore, and Mark (2020)

12 FOUND SOMETHING

Neither the police nor CeCe would reveal anything to us that was confidential to the case. They merely kept us informed in the simplest of terms as to what they could share with our family. However, the information they did provide was important and extremely helpful as it continued to reinforce our hope.

In December of 2021 we learned from the police that CeCe found **something...** My family prayed that we would someday soon receive answers!

On January 11th, 2022, we received an email from Detective Ogawa.

"Carol, although I cannot go into too many details... CeCe is very knowledgeable and experienced in her field and the information she provided has potential... **We have requested the assistance of the FBI, and are currently awaiting approval...** *Keep in mind, though, that even if we can obtain the sample we are looking for, there is no guarantee that the person we are looking at is the suspect..."*

Later that day Carol received a phone call from Detective Ogawa. He said the FBI *is* involved and that he just received a message from the "Reno *Police Department"* ....someone will be following the suspect (to obtain his abandoned DNA).

WOW!

The murder suspect is still *Alive* and living in Reno, *Nevada* (of all places) and **he's being *followed*** by Detective Moon's shadow!

I emailed CeCe and she replied:

"Wow is right! As I may have mentioned previously, I had to use an unconventional approach due to the lack of strong match data. If it works, it will be a first of sorts… As far as him being alive, I have the chorus of an old Billy Joel song running through my head.

#onlythegooddieyoung… Sending my best, - CeCe".

So true. This guy (if it is him) brutally killed our sister when she was barely 19 and he must now be in his 70's. Nancy never had the opportunity to go to college, get married, have children, pursue a career, and simply live life, yet he's still out there *somewhere*.

The city of Reno is in the northwest section of the state of Nevada, along the Nevada-California border. It sits about **22** miles from Lake Tahoe and is known as *"The Biggest Little City in the World"*. It's also the same state where our mom passed away and where Carol, Mark, and CeCe first met.

It's strange to think that after 50 years something so small and deep inside the killer's cells, something that can't even be seen directly by the human eye, may have revealed clues to his identity. His 50/50 mix of parental information provided just enough to get one match in a DNA database. Each segment of DNA (located on specific areas of an individual chromosome) is like a unique *yellow brick* that laid together in its entirety creates a detailed *roadmap*.

Seeing this limited data through her liquid-crystal display (LCD) computer monitor (or let's just call it a *crystal ball*), was CeCe able to build a family tree of the suspected killer's relatives? Was the family *tree* CeCe created *talking to her* and *throwing a few apples* of information? Does it show her where this *yellow brick road* leads? Somewhere on this long and winding road the killer resides. No longer translucently invisible, he's finally being pursued by other heroes in this story. I too have song lyrics in my head,

> "I'm bein' followed by a moonshadow" and
> "Let It Snow, Let It Snow, Let It Snow!"

What is *Abandoned DNA*? It's basically any amount of human tissue capable of DNA analysis that was discarded willfully, inadvertently, or involuntarily, by a person (but not by police coercion). Once obtained, it will be analyzed to see if it's a 100% match compared to the DNA on the blue towel that was left at the crime scene. If it is, then *he* is the murderer (based on overwhelming genetic evidence).

The laws regarding the use of DNA in violent crimes by the police continue to evolve. Hopefully it will prevail, leaning in favor of justice. It's not only helping to find murderers and violent offenders, but it's also vindicating and removing the wrongfully convicted from prison.

DNA does not change over time regarding its use in profile identification. It basically remains the same no matter if you're age 1 or 100. DNA does not lie and *cuts to the truth*!

The average human body is made up of about 30 trillion cells. We shed around 500 million of these skin cells every day, as well as leave behind nearly 40 to 100 hairs per day. We can also spew around 3,000 droplets containing our cells with every single sneeze we make.   If you are alive on this earth, you're leaving a *yellow brick trail* of DNA.

Police will look for anything that was *discarded* by the suspect that might contain DNA such as a Styrofoam coffee cup, cigarette butt, tissue paper, a *witch's broom handle*, etc. The more active a person is in this world, the more opportunities there are. It can take time, but police who are trained in this area are patient, creative, and resourceful.

They are looking for the right opportunity that presents itself, at the right place and time. We are hopeful that they will soon have their opportunity. I have never prayed for someone to be *sloppy* and abandon part of their physical being until now.

I have been told over the years that the murderer is *more than likely dead* (which was highly probable). Yet I knew this was no reason to sit idly by and do nothing. If he is still alive, he needs to be pulled off the streets so that this hopefully never happens to someone else's sister, mother, or daughter. With the new knowledge that he *has* been alive for the last 50 years, I'm now concerned that this *may* be the case.

No matter how you count, it took most of my entire lifetime or to be exact: a half century, 50 years, 600 months, or more simply put 18,250 days to get to a point where it's now possible to resolve Nancy's murder.

The essential meaning of *"determination"* is to continue trying to do or achieve something that is difficult. I believe our family (and CeCe) have been more than determined.

The technological advancement needed during these last 50 years to feasibly solve Nancy's cold case were immense. It was not until the 1970s when fully programmable desktop computers arrived. The introduction of DNA testing in the late 1970s and early 1980s eventually led scientists to create even more powerful tests for identification of biological relationships.

In 1992 internet access was made available for the public and its use rapidly expanded. DNA testing for family historians became available on a commercial basis in the year 2000. In 2003, scientists announced that the human genome had been sequenced with an accuracy of 99.99%. And, of course, the new science of *genetic genealogy* began. These, among many other developments linked together, were necessary to achieve this feat.

The span of time and the advancements in technology has been enormous. It has taken a *basket full* of patience, prayers, determination, technology, and teamwork. Now armed with all these attributes we seem to be nearing our destination.

If Nancy's case is solved, it will be the oldest cold case murder to date in the history of Hawaii resulting in a conviction and one of the oldest in the nation.

13 ANOTHER DIRECTION

March 11th, 2022 (3 months later)

CeCe, we just received this reply from the Honolulu police:

"Carol, there have been no developments since I last emailed you. The agency we are working with has not been successful in obtaining the sample we requested. They have made their best efforts and are continuing to try..." - Detective Ogawa

Thoughts?

Reply: "They can't get a court order on GG (genetic genealogy) analysis alone. **I have another idea that I will reach out to them about.** I sent the detective an email just now with my idea. I hope it helps! Thanks for forwarding the update!" -CeCe

Later that afternoon...

"Hi CeCe, we just heard from Detective Ogawa. He mentioned that the laws in Hawaii regarding collecting DNA are much stricter than in Nevada (so this was a concern). The amount of man hours required are significant due to someone having to be involved following this person 24/7. He mentioned that the suspect has "many relatives" (as I'm sure you know) so they are going a different direction by asking one of these relatives to volunteer to give a sample. (Thank you for guiding them in this direction). It sounds like this may be a much faster avenue! We cannot thank you enough CeCe for all your help"! - Jack

A *"large extended family"* … I know what that's all about. In this case the suspect's large family would more than likely be a liability rather than an asset.

The percentage of those asked to help solve a missing person or violent crime (even if it involves a family member) is just over 70 percent. And if one member declines, another may just do so. The larger the family, the greater the odds. I like the odds! However, in a court of law, a match through genetic genealogy is taken as a very good tip and not probable cause.

Investigative Genetic Genealogy can also use *"Target Testing"* as a tool (also referred to as *"Kinship Testing"*) to zero in on a suspect. In this case, testing the DNA of a living relative residing on the family genealogy tree, by someone who is willing to voluntarily submit their DNA. In doing so, they can help solve a violent crime, identify a missing person, etc. The risk, however, is the suspect may be alerted if the volunteer does not keep the test confidential.

If the DNA that was freely given by a family member proves to be closely related to the DNA found on the blue towel, it will help the cause of obtaining a court order. This also means no more following the suspect waiting for something to be discarded as abandoned DNA. Once a court order is obtained, the police can *"take"* his DNA even if he does not agree.

When Dorothy asks herself, *"which way is the Emerald City?"*, the Scarecrow replies *"that way is a very nice way!"* while pointing in **2** different confusing directions. CeCe creatively discovered the correct direction to proceed.

On Thursday, May 12th, 2022, my wife and I were visiting Arlington, Virginia (not far from the United States Air Force Memorial). It was there that I received a text from Carol: *"I just got this email!!!"*

"Carol, they were successful in collecting a sample from the family member and it has been tested with **encouraging results**. We now are strategizing the best way to legally obtain a sample from the actual subject. We are currently conferring with our prosecutors and are working on a plan for this. - Detective Ogawa"

After Half a Century, We Finally Got Him!!!

Our emotions ran deep and wide. For most of our lifetime, we were afraid this day would never arrive! I was a boy of 12 going on 13 when Nancy was killed, and now I'm a 63-year-old man. This new information was more than a good sign.

CeCe's reply to my email after informing her of the information we just received from the police:

"I am so glad the detective gave you the update. I am, of course, thrilled (but not surprised) that my hypothesis was valid. I think we should expect that it will take some time for them to build the case and do what they need to do to make sure things stick. (This guy is sneaky, and I am sure he thinks himself very clever.)

Remember, the work I do is only considered a "tip" and they need to do their full investigation and find evidence outside of the lead I provided, most importantly, the direct match to the STR profile on file for Nancy's case. We are slowly progressing (and made a big jump forward), but we aren't there quite yet. So, you all will need to be patient a little while longer. Sending lots of love to you all, - CeCe Moore"

CeCe is, of course, correct. Additionally, something deep inside my ancestral DNA also tells me, **this is the guy!**
If this information is all that is ever achieved from all this hard work, and all these years, then today is a *victory for Nancy* and the *land of OZ*. For the 1st time in over 50 years, Carol and I talked about moving beyond detectives (crime scene, cold case, and digital genetic genealogy detectives) to judges, lawyers, and the *gears* of the larger legal system. A prosecuting attorney will soon be putting to good use all the hard work the detectives and CeCe have accomplished.

And we will be there to *apply oil* to these gears as needed.

We know there is more work to be done and this guy is not yet arrested or charged with any crime. Our family still doesn't know his name or anything about him, however *"they"* do. The police in **2** states, the FBI, CeCe and her team, and soon a judge or **2** will also know enough to issue a warrant.

Follow up email: *"Hi Jack, ...this one is a bit more complex, however since the STR match isn't to his own surreptitious DNA sample, but rather to a close family member that matched at the right relationship level. I imagine the judge will approve the warrant for an arrest under the circumstances, but I am not 100% sure. It could be possible that the warrant is just to collect the DNA sample from him... -CeCe".*

Obtaining his actual DNA and comparing it against the DNA abandoned at the crime scene over 50 years ago, is now just a matter of paperwork, procedure, and the brave effort of the police. We are convinced it will be a 100% match.

We Got Him!

14 PATIENCE

Email from Detective Ogawa June 8th, 2022

"Carol, ...This would be the first case in Hawaii in which an arrest could be made as a result of genetic genealogy, so there is no case precedence on which to base legal decisions. I know you are eager for results, but we need to tread carefully so as not to make bad case law that could affect future investigations involving GG (Genetic Genealogy). Thank you for your patience. - Detective Ogawa"

Carol and I agree that Nancy's case was instrumental in getting Hawaii's 1st DNA testing lab, CODIS certification, and their 1st cold case unit, so it's understandable that her case would also be their 1st potential arrest using GG. We are encouraged that they are being extra careful on Nancy's case (so this sticks) and for all future cases. Even though we would like to see things move quicker, we understand the historic legal importance this is for the State of Hawaii, so it's worth waiting a bit longer.

Once again, all we can really do is have patience. Patience is a virtue. However, as a family, we continue to push forward as needed! I admit that I'm feeling the pressure of time as none of us are getting any younger. All nine of us are now long in years, yet we are still here, and we really want answers before we lose anyone else. I'm afraid time may be running out.

However, we seem to be stuck in the bureaucracy of red tape, so Carol and I decided it was time to call the prayer warriors into action. We need the entire family's help! Carol sent out a family group text message:

(July 25th, 2022) *Brothers and Sisters, it's been more than 6 months since I last communicated with you concerning Nancy's case... It hasn't been easy for Jack and I to hold back some new information with you due to the sensitive nature... We need your help! Nancy's case is being held up because of legal barriers. I can't say what specifically they are except, at this point, all our prayers need to be focused on the legal issues involved so her case can move forward. I know that if we ALL pray for these legal barriers to be removed, it will happen... We are getting very close! Love you all, -Carol.*

We prayed, just like we did 57 years ago for snow!

Just like the card Nancy carried with her states: *"Love is the most universal, formidable, and mysterious of cosmic energies".* After praying together as a family, we soon received a *snowstorm* of answers that we never thought we would hear - an actual timeline of when an arrest would be made and it's all within the next **2** weeks! The red tape now seems to be resolved and God's timing is at hand.

CeCe couldn't find the killer within the family tree she created from the one hit she received after looking in several databases. The hit was from a relative who was just too distant to make a direct connection to him, so she had to get extremely creative and go a different route. She decided to try something that had never been done before. Her inspiration was *pure genius*!

Armed with only a few unique biological markers within the DNA of the killer's blood, she reverse-engineered the typical approach genetic genealogists take. His DNA held **2** distinct sets of racial ancestral data: Italian (specifically Sicily) and Romanian. CeCe's new method was to attempt to exploit these facts.

CeCe also had a hunch the target murder suspect lived somewhere in the vicinity of where Nancy lived and worked at the time. She also knew that the percentage of the Sicilian – Romanians living in Waikiki Hawaii in 1972 would be extremely small in relation to the overall population.

But where to begin? Where do you look for a specific, yet unknown person who lived in Honolulu Hawaii 50 years ago, armed with only a few ancestral racial facts? If only there was a list somewhere where you can look up Sicilian – Romanian last names of people who lived there at the time. **There is!** - CeCe turned to the public 1971 *Honolulu phone book* that is now available on the internet. (Genius!)

Yes, CeCe found the suspect in the phone book!

"Let your fingers do the walking" is a slogan from the 1970's for using the Yellow and White Page phone books. The slogan was made famous in the phone company's advertisements. It was the best way to find what and who you were looking for back in the day, and its exactly what CeCe did!

Please don't misunderstand, the alleged killer was not simply listed under "murderers" in alphabetical order of last names in the phone book. CeCe spent countless hours with enormous patience eliminating all the names that could *not* possibly be Sicilian or Romanian. This eventually left her with a short list of possible Sicilian – Romanians living in Honolulu in 1971-1972. With this information it was then a matter of researching and building a family tree for each person on the short list to confirm if they contained both specific ancestral racial lineages she was looking for.

This eventually led her to only one person who was a male, of the right age, living in Honolulu Hawaii early in 1972, who had both Sicilian and Romanian family lineages. The old phone book's white pages not only provide names, but it also provides physical home addresses. The suspect's home address was near both Nancy's home and place of work! (#537-1082 / 1050 Kinau St, Honolulu HI.)

In addition to being a brilliant genetic genealogist CeCe is also an extremely effective digital detective. She is well versed in using all the online information available on the internet such as social media, news articles, (and yes) old phone books.

Having the name of one person who has all the correct genetic ancestral traits that match the assumed killer's DNA profile, as well as the right time, and place, is still not enough. CeCe needed even more information to be able to go to the police with a viable *"tip"*.

By researching the suspect's history, CeCe was able to see documented life events of the suspect that are consistent with violent criminal behavior. These events included violence towards his wife (who eventually divorced him) and a girlfriend (who he attempted to rape). The sum-total of all this information provided CeCe a solid *"tip"* that was worthy of handing over to the Honolulu cold case detectives.

The police agreed the tip had merit, so they requested (after obtaining a warrant) that the Reno police follow the suspect to gather any abandoned DNA. The Reno police spent many hours attempting to follow him to obtain any discarded DNA samples. However, the suspect rarely left his home.

Eventually the police forewarned Carol and I that the time-cost in manhours alone was becoming extremely impractical. The Honolulu Police were relying upon an external law enforcement agency that was not under their control. They also had to be very careful that the Reno Police followed Hawaii state laws in these matters as Nevada laws were more laxed in their approach to the collection of DNA, which could adversely affect a trial. This precaution only added more delays.

It seemed as if the suspect was profoundly aware of how law enforcement approaches the collection of this type of biological information. His actions seemed to be deliberately guarded so this method was eventually deemed impractical.

The Fourth Amendment guarantees *"the right of the people to be secure in their persons, houses, papers, and effects, against unreasonable searches and seizures."* Typically, a *"search"* is interpreted to require probable cause and a warrant (which Hawaii has granted) or, at a minimum, individualized suspicion. Most court's view collecting and analyzing DNA as a *"search"* in Fourth Amendment challenges of the use of DNA databases. However, not all jurisdictions have definitively settled the legal status of pre-conviction in the use of DNA samplings.

It is currently unlawful to simply confront a suspect and forcefully take their DNA. Civil rights are always a consideration (and rightly so). However, following this suspect was simply not working.

So, what else can be done?

15 SINS OF THE FATHER (WITCHES)

Once CeCe created the suspect's family tree and researched his public information, she also discovered that he had a son and two daughters. This information revealed there was a clear falling-out between his ex-wife and children (an estranged relationship). CeCe had a hunch that maybe there would be some cooperation with his children if they were asked to voluntarily give their DNA to help solve a violent crime. She recommended to the police that they contact one of the children (now grown adults) to provide a DNA sample. The police agreed.

Every so often there are moments in life where the relationship between a father and son is strained and measured, yet action must be taken (not words), even if it sends a message of condemnation. The DNA sample of the close family member was provided by the suspect's *biological son*!

When the police approached his son (John) and asked if he would voluntarily help solve a violent crime he simply said: *"This is about my biological father, isn't it?"* John gladly and freely gave his DNA. Once John's DNA was processed, it was completely consistent with his biological father's. It was a match! (a notable *parental DNA match*) Scientifically, the suspect found in the phone book matches the killer based on the DNA evidence.

I'm not an expert in DNA, however it's clear to me that DNA is a true recordkeeper of every individual human's collective ancestral biological history. However, DNA does not record the sins of the father. God allows each of us, every day we have on this earth, the free will to make decisions on how we approach whatever we encounter in life.

DNA does not predetermine if you will choose good over evil. Decisions of good or evil are ours to make. At some point it's no longer a nurture / nature debate but rather a choice (free will). John chose **good and righteousness** and is to forever be commended for his brave and honorable action that day. I am of the belief that he did this as much or more for his own mother and family than he did for ours. Either way, my family is forever grateful!

The serendipitous repeating of the number **"2"** has long held significant meaning to my family ever since Nancy was murdered (for example, Nancy's favorite television show was a series called *"Room 222"*). Some people say the meaning of the number **2** suggests it: *"symbolizes long-lasting, meaningful, and strong relationships"*. Others say it means: *"balance, peace, faith, and endurance"*. (How about simply: *"Faith and endurance to find peace in a strong relationship?"*) Maybe so... I'm just not sure about this kind of mystical tea-reading stuff. All I know is we keep seeing it pop-up in unusual frequency.

We again find it strange that on September 1**2**th, **2**022, at **2:22**pm a **Warrant of Arrest** was issued for the murder of Nancy Anderson of **2222** Aloha Drive on January 7th, 197**2**, and signed by Judge James Kawashima of the State of Hawaii. **(Day 18,512)**

Subscribed and sworn to before me this __12th__ day of **September, 2022** at __2:22__ a.m./p.m.

JAMES S. KAWASHIMA

JUDGE OF THE ABOVE-ENTITLED COURT
STATE OF HAWAII

There can be moments in life where you find the thing you were afraid of most is *not* really all that scary. In fact, it can end up being downright pathetic. If you ever get the chance to face your demons, no matter how long, difficult, or small the task is, *I highly recommend* **DO THAT!**

On September 13th, 2022, around 4 a.m. Hawaii time, police in Reno, Nevada, arrested 77-year-old **"Tudor** (pronounced *"2"-door*) **Chirila"** on suspicion of second-degree murder. Tudor is now incarcerated in jail while pending extradition to Hawaii for the murder of our sister 50 years ago. His world has now *crashed to the floor* and *shattered* into many small, sharp, and not so kind objects with no one left in his life to help clean up his mess. Our mysterious *riddle,* however, has finally unraveled.

The murder defendant, now looking *broken and brittle,* was booked into jail in Reno, Nevada on September 14th, 2022.

CHIRILA, TUDOR JR
Booking Number: 2210713
Age: 77
JID Number: P00190466
Booking Date: 09/14/2022

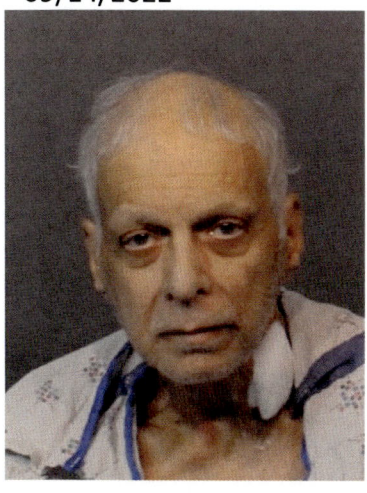

As citizens we expect those who work for the justice system to be honest people, of good character, fighting for law and order (Knights in shining armor). As **Glinda states in the Wizard of Oz**: *"Are You a Good Witch or a Bad Witch?"* Tudor Chirila was a rare and wicked Bad Witch. We never imagined in all our speculative scenarios that our unfortunate journey for justice would lead us to a *Bad Witch of justice*.

In 1972 **Tudor** was a graduate assistant at the University of Hawaii, Mānoa. He was married at the time of Nancy's murder and owned a car, possibly allowing him to disappear into thin air. Nancy worked at a local restaurant not far from her apartment. She lived and worked between where **Tudor** lived (1050 Kinau St.), worked (University of Hawaii), and played (Waikiki Beach).

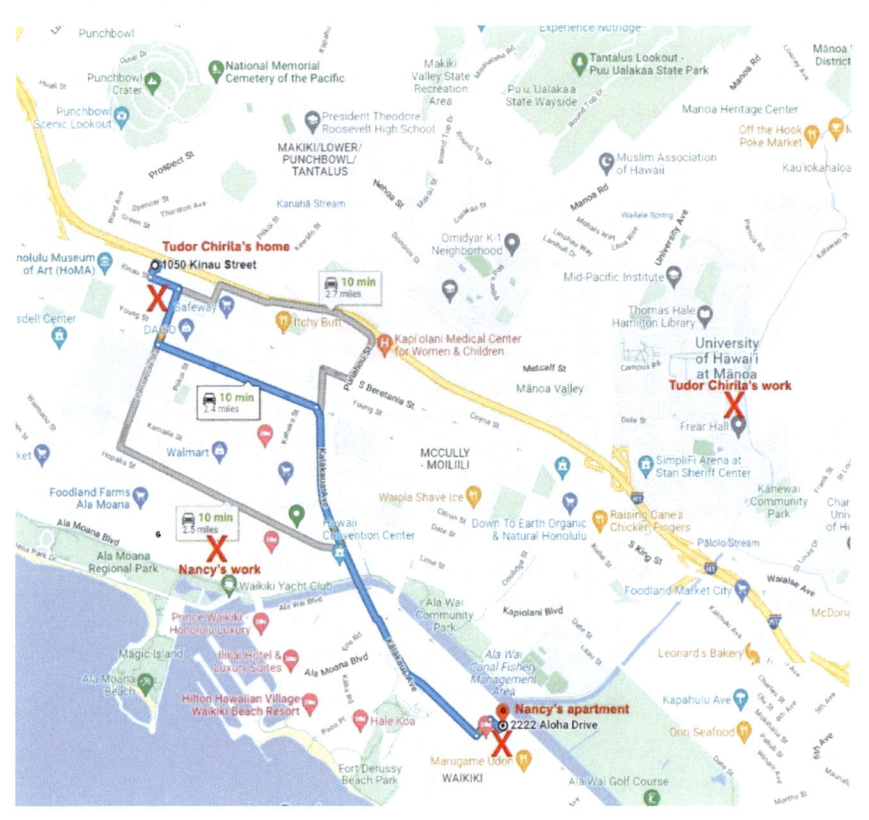

Sometime after potentially murdering our sister, he eventually left Hawaii and earned his law degree from the Pacific McGeorge School of Law in Sacramento, California. In 1978 he was admitted to practice law in Nevada and became Nevada's chief deputy attorney general in 1980 and a deputy attorney general in 1981.

He was also a senior assistant to the Reno City Attorney in 1986-87 and in 1994 he ran for the Nevada Supreme Court (and lost). He was reportedly arrested in the middle of his campaign for not paying over $33,000 in child support. The next year, prosecutors reportedly dropped charges against him alleging he kidnapped his girlfriend with the intent to rape her.

Reno Gazette-Journal, Saturday, September 3, 1994

POLITICS

Underdog spends no money but thinks he'll do well in Supreme Court race

By Mike Henderson
GAZETTE-JOURNAL

DECISION '94

Tudor Chirila is the clear underdog in Tuesday's Nevada Supreme Court race against incumbent Bob Rose and Clark County District Judge Myron Leavitt.

While Rose and Leavitt have taken to the airwaves with expensive commercials, Chirila hasn't spent a dime on his campaign.

The 49-year-old Carson City lawyer hasn't solicited so much as a dollar.

And last weekend Chirila finished serving an eight-day jail sentence for being in arrears on child support.

Still, he thinks he'll do well in the election, "perhaps as a protest vote candidate," he said.

"I feel there are a lot of people upset with the present candidates and I thought I would be an alternative candidate for people who want to protest but not vote for 'none of the above'," Chirila said.

He served the jail sentence on a contempt citation for failing to pay more than $33,000 in child support. He didn't appeal, he said, because the Supreme Court ignores his appeals.

He contested a court order requiring him to pay $995 a month in child support. Deputy District Attorney Trina Dahlin said Chirila ducked his child-support responsibilities, paying only $150 a month for their support.

"My position," Chirila said, "is that the alleged child-support arrearages are the product of gross judicial impropriety."

He contends his trial judge left the bench during a hearing, talked to Chirilla's wife and lawyer outside Chirilla's presence, then returned to the bench.

Chirilla contends he didn't know what the arrearages were until he received a court order. His request for a new trial, he said, has been pending since 1992.

Meanwhile, he said, he's been seeking an accounting of the arrearages.

"I think a full accounting will show that there are zero arrearages," he said.

In 1998, Tudor filed suit against the owner "Joe Conforte" of the infamous Nevada Mustang Ranch brothel, seeking $14 million in damages. In a federal indictment that year, U.S. prosecutors in Reno identified Tudor as the former president of A.G.E. Corp., a company that served as a front for Conforte.

The Mustang Ranch is about 20 miles east of Reno located in Sparks, Nevada. Under past owner Joe Conforte, the Mustang Ranch became Nevada's first licensed brothel in 1971. This eventually led to the legalization of brothels in 10 of 17 counties in the state of Nevada. The Mustang Ranch opened to the public in 1971 and was America's largest brothel with 166 acres and the most profitable.

When he testified as a government witness, Tudor acknowledged he knew the corporation was owned and controlled by Conforte, who was believed to be a fugitive in South America when the case went to trial in 1999. Conforte was also reportedly connected with organized crime and was sometimes called the Godfather of legal prostitution. Conforte reportedly controlled most organized crime in Northwestern Nevada. The Mustang Ranch was eventually sold to another company that was later found to be a subsidiary of the offshore A.G.E. Corporation of which Joe was the main shareholder.

Even though Tudor was once a chief deputy attorney general, he ended up neck deep with organized MOB crime in Nevada as a *Bad Witch*. He also possessed the knowledge of the law which gave him insight on how to evade exposure and delay capture for murder that allowed him to be *invisible* all these years.

He was highly educated, married, and employed at the University of Hawaii as a graduate assistant at the time of Nancy's murder.

It's not hard to understand why Nancy may have trusted him.

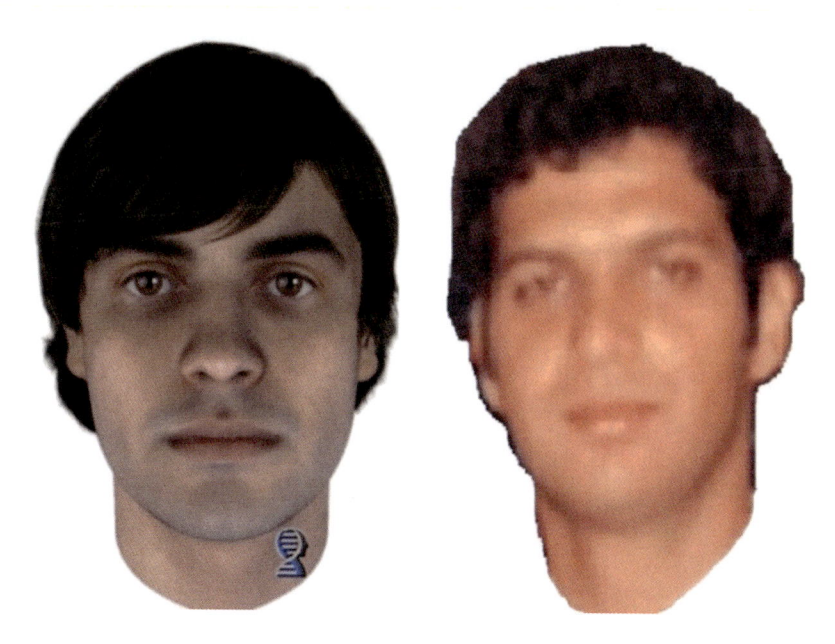

Tudor Chirila 1960-70s

Above (L) is the Snapshot DNA Phenotyping digital image created from the murderer's DNA, obtained from the blood he left on the blue towel taken from Nancy's apartment in 1972.

Above (R) is a photo of Tudor Chirila (from the late 1960's early 1970's), as he looked around the time of Nancy's murder.

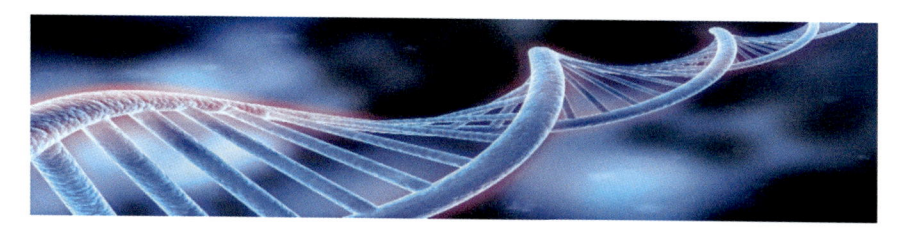

The double helix of DNA

16 TRUTH AND JUSTICE

Every so often there are moments in life where the love between siblings is immeasurable and a message of standing united together must be demonstrated using all the words of faith and prayer.

On September 15th, 2022, we traveled from around the country (Gail and Jim via video conference), for yet another family reunion and to attend Tudor Chirila's first trial in Reno, Nevada. We (The Andersons) were there for Nancy, to bear witness for her Justice! Marty was also invited and attended via video conference.

The Anderson family praying for justice

The Anderson family
Mike, Carol, Nancy (photo), Mary, Betty, Jack, Janet, and Bill *Gail and Jim not pictured

On December 2nd, 2022, Tudor was extradited from Nevada and flown to Hawaii in handcuffs, escorted by 2 Honolulu Police Officers. I believe it will be difficult for Tudor to sweep away the truth about Nancy's brutal murder or provide a rational defense of how his blood got on our sister's bathroom towel that day back in 1972. However, we can only hope and pray once again for justice through a *conviction*, which is never guaranteed.

The wheels of justice turn slowly, and we know better than most! Nevertheless, they are now turning extremely slowly for Tudor, who we believe murdered our sister. He's sitting in a jail back in Honolulu where he belongs (with no scenic views), watching the rust grow, and the paint dry until an official trial date is determined.

On July 11th, 2023, we learned that a similar cold case trial in Hawaii just concluded. This case involved a murder that took place in in 1982, 10 years after Nancy's murder. The jury returned a *"not guilty"* verdict and the deputy public defender stated: *"The case was built on DNA that ... I mean, anybody can have DNA. The bottom line is they didn't have enough (other) evidence."*

Of course, anyone can have DNA... (Everyone has DNA!) However, that doesn't mean everyone's DNA is everywhere. It's the way the DNA was found and associated with the crime. In Tudor's case, the DNA was obtained from blood evidence where both the victim and the defendant's fresh blood were located on the same objects at the murder scene at the same time. We can only pray that this is enough and/or there is other additional supporting evidence for a conviction.

We are certain this recent verdict will not slip by Tudor or his public defense attorney.

We expect it will be a point of contention at his trial and find this news unsettling as it poses yet again another *roadblock*. We also hope a new precedence has not been set in the State of Hawaii that will favor future cases such as Tudor's.

There is a legal term known as *"Consciousness of Guilt"* that could possibly come into play. A consciousness of guilt may, for example, be exhibited by a false alibi or explanation for one's actions, intimidation of a witness, destruction or concealment of evidence or **flight**. (as in *flying on a broomstick*).

When the Reno police went to Tudor's apartment (unit #**22**1) to obtain his DNA once the warrant was issued, they could not arrest him until *after* the results came back from the lab and *only* if the results proved to be a match (which it was). They were required by law to give him the warrant, which stated they were taking his DNA as he was a *"suspect in the murder of Nancy Anderson in Hawaii in 1972"*.

This, however, left the police with a dilemma as they had to leave the suspect alone and free for a few days. All they could do was observe his apartment building from a distance and follow him if he did run. The timing issue is an unfortunate gap in our current legal system. This absence of the law is why Carol and I had the family pray months ago. We prayed for the removal of this red tape (which gave the police pause) as we were cautioned that a *flight risk* was a real possibility.

83

Tudor, armed with the knowledge that he has been accused after all these years, did what might be considered an act of *"Consciousness of Guilt"*. He went to his neighbor who lived next **door** in unit #**222** (of all places) and gave away his car title and last few remaining possessions from his troubled life and said, **"they are coming back to arrest me"**.

Tudor then consumed a massive number of drugs and tried to burn his apartment building down (like setting his **broom stick on fire**). Once the fire department arrived, it took more than **a bucket of water** to put the flames out. The paramedics hauled him off to a hospital where he nearly **died by melting** his brain in a drug overdose. Once the DNA results came back as a *"positive match"* and Tudor recovered from his attempted suicide, the police arrested him in his hospital room.

I'm not a legal expert, however, we are hopeful that his actions in response to the accusation is considered a *"Consciousness of Guilt"* as well as arson and attempted murder of others in the building. Who would ever do such a thing if they knew they were completely innocent? His reaction to the news seems like a desperate and over the top attempt to evade justice. We hope these facts of events are admissible in court as we may need all the *other evidence* we can get!

We find it yet again spiritually strange that the suspect of a murder committed at **2222** Aloha Drive in Honolulu, gave away his last few earthly possessions to a neighbor at a different **222** apartment in Reno, over a distance of **2,500** miles and 50 years. This revelation and Tudor's attempted **Hollywood ending** are shocking, yet it's also a very natural conclusion for those of us who have been on this very long and prolonged journey for justice.

17 HOME

We have since learned that Tudor's parents and sister lived in the Portland, Oregon area for many years. In fact, within 30 minutes from where I lived with my wife and children for many decades and only *2* miles away from where I worked. I'm sure he must have visited them from time to time. He was *much closer* than I ever imagined!

The truth is often obtained from the simplest of things, yet gleaning its natural secrets can take an immense amount of time and hard work. That old blue towel from Nancy's apartment was from a set of towels our mom gifted to Nancy, when she moved out of our house back in 1971. We find it incredible that from *2* critical pieces of evidence: one of those 50-year-old towels and a very old phone book, CeCe got the accused killer's face, family tree, and freedom!

We waited 1 year and *2* months for the State of Hawaii to set a firm trial date, however the defense attorney kept delaying for various reasons. One of the main reasons was a request by the defense that more time was needed to get up to speed on the use of DNA and the new forms of Investigative Genetic Genealogy. We were informed that delay is a *standard* defensive tactic, especially when a strong defense is lacking. The Judge granted these requests so that an appeal or mistrial does not favor the defendant (which for us would be horrific).

Time never grows old, just those of us standing in its wake feel its force as we age. Justice was served on *Christmas Day* 2023. Tudor Chirila died *2* weeks prior to the 52nd anniversary of Nancy's murder. There were no presents waiting for him under the Christmas tree. (It had nothing to do with the absence of snow for Santa to land his sleigh.)

It seems as if the ghost of Nancy's Christmas past, present, and future, caught up with him in the end.

On December 25th (Day 19,345) at 7:46 pm Chirila was pronounced dead at the Queen's Medical Center in Honolulu. He was transported to the hospital from the local jail for comfort measures and end of life care. According to the police report, he had not eaten, drank, or taken necessary medication for *2* days prior to his death (and apparently had tongue cancer). The cause of death was cardiac arrest and there were no signs of life trauma or foul play. He died incarcerated, broke, and stained with the stigma of a murderer.

It's ironic that he failed to commit suicide by consuming a massive number of drugs just prior to his arrest, then dies a year later due to the lack of needed medication prior to his trial. I can't help but think his last thoughts were: *"Who would have thought a good little girl like you could destroy my beautiful wickedness?"* – (Last words of the Wicked Witch of the West / The Wizard of Oz).

A person cannot be convicted of murder after they die, however, a case can be closed as *"solved"* if a dead person is determined to be the killer (for example through DNA). In our case, we received the Christmas gift of a *"solved cold case"* with Tudor Chirila named as the murderer with no possibility of a long messy trial, an appeal, mistrial, or him getting off the hook through a technicality. He spent the last miserable year of his life behind bars.

On January *2*nd, 2024, (exactly 5*2* years from when Nancy returned to Hawaii) we were invited to attend a video conference presentation by the District Attorney for a briefing on the conclusion of Tudor's case.

We learned that we may never know the reason he killed Nancy, if other coconspirators were involved, or any other answers surrounding that day and we're not waiting another 50 years to find out. We will leave these questions to others to pursue if they're even in the realm of possibilities. All we know is we got the answer to our principal question... *Who killed Nancy Anderson?* – Based on all the significant scientific forensic genetic evidence, *Tudor Chirila killed our sister!*

We did everything within our power in seeking justice for Nancy. My family and I have traveled a lifelong journey cleaning up the shards of glass from a horrific event thrown at our feet. Many years ago, as a 12-year-old boy at Nancy's funeral, I made a secret vow to God, Nancy, and to myself, that I would never stop until this day arrived. I'm now a 64-year-old man and our task is finally complete so, I too, can rest in peace.

Nancy's murder is the oldest murder case to date in Hawaii resulting in an indictment. Older solved cases involved murderers, and the victim's immediate family members, who were already deceased. Nancy's murder is also the 5th oldest cold case in the nation resulting in an indictment and the oldest case in the world involving the largest number of immediate family members still surviving (based on the time of this publication). However, we would have greatly preferred never having to be a part of any unfortunate statistics like this.

Going forward, those who commit violent crimes not only need to be concerned about their abandoned DNA or any family member contributing their DNA to a database, but they now also need to worry about the simple nature of their own name.

Thanks to a new groundbreaking Investigative Genetic Genealogy method developed by CeCe.

We are more than grateful to get much needed help! Good people like an angel named CeCe Moore, many detectives, and other *Good Deed Doers*, who cared enough to join our journey and help solve our lifelong mystery. It took over a half century to find *the answers we were looking for* and return to the *altar of OZ* to receive our reward.

We *did not surrender* in our quest for the truth and like the song *Moon Shadow* states: *"Did it take long to find me?"* (Yes… yes it certainly did!)

I have faith that someday each one of us will leave this world and meet up with loved ones once again, who are waiting for us on the other side. When it's my turn, I hope to greet Nancy, our mom, and our dad, and say *"we all played our part and did everything possible to bring justice for Nancy"* (a promise kept and mission complete).

Our Dorothy needed to receive justice and the final word in this story. Her memory and place in our hearts is forever epic. Nancy is *a star in shining armor* who will never be forgotten, and to us, her story is legendary. She will forever be a part of our family and **Our Home**.

Our mysterious Brittle Riddle is finally solved!

EPILOGUE

I eventually retired from the Air Force and in my constant attempt to try and keep warm, moved to Arizona. (It was the practical thing to do!) Detective Moon and many others who have followed in his shadow, have long since retired. However, all nine of us (Nancy's *Munchkin*-siblings) are still here. Over the last half century, we have been on a lifelong quest to resolve what happened that day.

I don't claim to be a writer or a storyteller. All I know is this story was inside me and it needed to get out. I can honestly say that for the most part it wrote itself and *it* insisted that it be told in this way. It was deciphered through the lens of faith in a higher power, logic of genuine science, and the imaginary fantasy of a young kid. I always felt like I was recruited (more like drafted and directed) to put this real true-life, short story, written over a long time, into printed *words*.

When I look back over these last fifty plus years, I am very thankful for every moment I've had with my family. We learned at a very young age about *good and evil*. The unfortunate truth is that there really are villains (*dragons and witches*) in this world, and yet our faith in God has never relented. He also places heroes (and *angels*) on this earth to help families like ours solve and clean up infamous mysteries such as the **BRITTLE RIDDLE** that was left at our feet. We can never thank those angels enough!

-Jack Anderson

Even though Nancy did not have a pair of *ruby slippers* at her feet to bring her safely *home* to us and I don't have *military medals* for your *hearts, minds, and bravery*, I do want to *point out* each one of you who were there to *play your part* over these many years.

Most of all my sister **Carol** and her husband **Mark** for all their hard work. We have worked very closely together for many years on Nancy's case. Carol and Mark took the lead on communicating with the Cold Case Detectives and represented our family (and helped with this story). They are amazing!

My **wife Edie, daughter Tiffany, and sons Heath and Nick**, who allowed me the time to pursue justice and write this story.

My brother **Mike**, who was forced to grow up much too soon, taking on difficult responsibilities, and having to deliver messages no parents should ever have to receive. He is always an inspirational example of honor, integrity, and courage.

My sister **Mary** for her encouragement and words of wisdom. Mary was very close to Nancy and knew her better than most in our family.

My entire family, life would not be the same without you. Thank you for your input in this story and helping to preserve our family history by *recalling what was revealed the day the music died*.

Marty, Nancy's best friend – Words can never express how much you meant to Nancy and our family. Thank you for being <u>our</u> friend!

All our **many friends and extended family** who over the years understood our quest and encouraged us to never give up hope.

The many Honolulu Police Officers and other legal professionals who were involved in Nancy's case over these 50 years. Without their efforts to collect and preserve critical evidence, as well as investigate every lead, this case would never have been able to move forward.

Detective Leslie Moon was the lead crime scene detective in 1972.

Detective Kruse who, at the age of 83 (1 of the last of **2** surviving crime scene detectives from 1972), testified in court that the blue towel which the DNA was obtained from was the same one found at the crime scene.

Chief of Police Francis Keala

Officer Milton Galase (1st responder to crime scene)

Officer George Gibbons (1st responder to crime scene)

Sergeant Henry Robinson (1st responder to crime scene)

Officer Robert Knight (1st responder to crime scene)

Lieutenant George Santos (1st responder to crime scene)

Major Arthur Dederick (1st responder to crime scene)

Detective William Mattson (1st responder to crime scene)

Detective Paul Trepte (1st responder to crime scene)

Detective Clement Enoka (1st responder to crime scene)

Major John Pekelo

Chief of Police Lee Donohue

Lieutenant Bill Kato

Detective Sergeant Clifford Rubio

Lieutenant Allen Napoleon

Detective Ken Higa

Captain Alan Arita

Detective Kathleen Osmond

Chief of Police Boisse P. Correa

Detective James V.L. Slayter

Captain Walter Ozeki

Detective Paul Okamoto

Detective Kelvin Hayakawa

Chief of Police Susan Ballard

Chief of Police **Arthur "Joe" Logan**

Detective Michael Ogawa Who worked diligently to obtain a conviction.

Judge James Kawashima of the State of Hawaii.

Amos Stege Chief Deputy District Attorney, Reno Nevada (Extradition Attorney).

Christopher Van Marter Assistant District Attorney, Honolulu Hawaii.

Scott Bell Deputy Prosecuting Attorney, Honolulu Hawaii.

Doreida R. O'Neill Victims advocate, Honolulu Hawaii.

The Brave Family Member "John" Who helped by providing the relative DNA sample.

Parabon NanoLabs and **Snapshot DNA Phenotyping Services.**

CeCe Moore who worked tirelessly to solve Nancy's case and to whom our family will always be eternally grateful. We pray that your *good work* will continue!

GOD for creating the most accurate and natural human identifier: **DNA**.

THANK YOU!

- FOR NANCY -

"Hearts will never be practical
until they can be made unbreakable."

-The Wizard of Oz

"The impractical things we do from the heart
make us human."

-Jack Anderson

OTHER NOTES:

2001: A friend of Carol and her husband Mark was a retired detective from Kona, Hawaii. After they told him Nancy's story, he strongly encouraged them to not give up but, instead, to contact the Chief of Police directly.

2005 meeting: During this meeting Mark and Carol were presented with some gifts and tokens representing Hawaii. They were treated with the utmost kindness and respect. At this time Carol presented Captain Arita a copy of the letter she wrote and personally handed to Boisse Correa, Chief of Police. In part it stated:

"We especially want to give credit and praise to Captain Arita. He has been not only professional and committed to solving this case, he has also treated our family with respect, concern, and kindness.......(he) has gone beyond what is expected and has shown the qualities of a true professional".

Credits / Reference:

Editor – *Carol Anderson Sampson*

Artist – *Nick Anderson* (cover art)

Artwork provided by – *Squadronposters.com – Anderson IP / LLC* *

Biography Information / Wikipedia - *CeCe Moore*

National Center for Health Statistics - *FBI's 2020 Uniform Crime Report*

Newspaper article - *Honolulu Star-Advertiser*

The Wizard of Oz (1939 film*) Metro-Goldwyn-Mayer* *quotes and references marked in *italic oblique type font.*

Song *"Moon Shadow"* by - *Cat Stevens*

Song *"American Pie"* by - *Don McLean*

Song *"Only the Good Die Young"* by - *Billy Joel*

Song "Let It Snow! Let It Snow! Let It Snow!" By - *Jule Styne and Sammy Cahn* (Best known sung by: Frank Sinatra, Dean Martin, and Jessica Simpson)

A male Witch is referred to as a – *Warlock* (just not in this story)

A few months after our dad was killed, our brother Mike (#1) interviewed one of dad's best friends and coworker (Roy Arthur Estep) who was there at the time of the accident that took our dad's life. Here is the article Mike wrote titled: "500 Building".

"500" BUILDING

It was a beautiful, beautiful day. The snow had just ceased falling and the ground was covered with a soft, white layer of fresh snow. The temperature outside was about twenty degrees above zero, but in the powerhouse it was the usual—about 110°F. Everyone was feeling exceptionally well. It's not unusual for our shift to feel wonderful, though. The number two shift has, for some time, been noted for its cheerfulness, dedication and true spirit of brotherhood. No other shift could compare to this high-flying and closely-knit team of eighty-five.

On Saturday the eighth of January, everyone was feeling just a little better than usual. We had just returned from our two days off and were all happy to be back together. However, there was one fellow who appeared a little happier and displayed a bigger smile than everyone else and that was the operator of Boiler # 18, Andy.

Since our boilers were adjacent, it was my privilege to have many long and interesting discussions with Andy. The topics ranged anywhere from my part-time job as a minister at a little church in Shephard, to the latest addition to Andy's home. I think I can honestly say that I visualized every segment of his addition as it was being built, even though I had never seen his house. Yes, Andy and I had many wonderful and worthwhile discussions and we knew each other better than brothers. Yes, and I knew just how special that Saturday was for Andy.

Earlier that very day, Andy had picked up his new suit—the suit he had to wait three years to get because he couldn't afford it. In fact, he even tried on his suit just before leaving for work that day, and his wife took a picture of him with her new camera, the Polaroid she had dreamed of for years, but which had become a reality only the day before. To add to this, Andy had just turned the next day in on vacation so that he and his wife could go out for dinner which for them was a very special occasion, and which they dared to do only twice a year. And finally, Andy knew that the new addition (his fourth) to his home was nearly completed. There were just a few touch-up jobs remaining. So, with all this in mind, that Saturday was a very special day for Andy.

Andy, who was never seen without a smile, who never said a mean word about anyone, who never spoke a single cuss word, was dutifully at work and was as dedicated as ever. At 6:00 P.M., two hours after reporting to work, Andy went downstairs for a cup of coffee and returned with his cup about two minutes later. I still had nearly a full cup or else I would have gone with him. Our desks were about one hundred feet apart, yet he smiled at me as he ascended the stairs behind his boiler and I returned my usual smile and then looked back at my panel board.

It couldn't have been thirty seconds when suddenly I heard several floor tubes crack beneath Andy's boiler. I immediately jumped up and dashed toward him. I hadn't gone five steps when his entire boiler (about forty feet long, thirty feet wide and seven stories high) exploded and the great pressure split open the corners of the boiler and buckled over the huge I-beams, and the steam and soot came bursting forth with great force. All this steam, soot and hot water went flying right before me. If I had been but two steps closer, I would have been right in it. I felt my heart leap. I knew Andy was in there—someplace, but I could not see him, in fact I couldn't even see my hand in front of my face. Yet Andy was in there and I had to find him. I yelled, "Andy, Andy, where are you?" And there was no reply. And so I yelled again as loud as I could, "Andy, Andy," and still no reply.

It was at this point that our foreman, Streider, came up to me and asked, "Roy, is Andy still in there?" And I yelled, "Yes, and I can't get through." Streider then said, "The only way we can hope to reach him is through the fire escape door on the other side." With that, Streider darted across the room and headed out the main door in an effort to reach the fire escape by circling the building.

I realized that that would take too long, but the only other way was to go right through the soot and steam. For me, this was the greatest moment and the greatest decision of my life. I dashed to the front wall and slowly felt my way along. I couldn't see a thing, not even the windows which were right next to me, yet I just had to keep moving, despite the fact that my face and ears were burnt. In a few seconds I reached the panel board and felt around until I found the coal-supply valve. I immediately turned it off, thus preventing the danger of another explosion and also slowing the outpour of steam. But I still couldn't find Andy and I asked myself where he might be. It was at that very moment that I felt a hand on my shoulder. I knew who it was. Andy, even though fatally burned, had come to the panel board to shut off the coal-supply.

I could see a little now and I led Andy to the fire escape where we met Streider, but as soon as Andy stepped onto the landing, the bitter coldness of the winter evening bit into his deeply burnt body. He quickly and wisely came back inside. Andy then quietly said that he was cold; so, without delay, we gently placed a blanket over his shoulders. By this time the ambulance was downstairs, so we (Streider and I) led him to the other stairway, located behind his boiler. He walked down the double flight by himself and on the way he said, "Tell them I'm a diabetic! I'm a diabetic! Remember." After he reached the foot of the stairs, he climbed into the ambulance without anyone's support.

I watched, helpless and bewildered, as the ambulance drove off with the man I loved because of our closeness, the man I admired because of his courage, and the man I respected because of his faith.

Today I still keep going back to my boiler, but it will never be the same. Our #2 shift is as quiet and lifeless as could possibly be. Everytime I look around while at work, I easily realize that there is someone missing; someone who put great spirit into our building, someone who was never seen without a smile, who never spoke an ill word about anyone, who never spoke a single cuss word and who will never be forgotten by me and the other members of the second shift in the "500" Building.

Michael Anderson

OTHER PHOTOS:

Nancy age 2 - 3   Anderson sisters (Nancy center)

The Andersons (Nancy far left / Easter 1960)

The Andersons (Nancy top center / Christmas 1965)

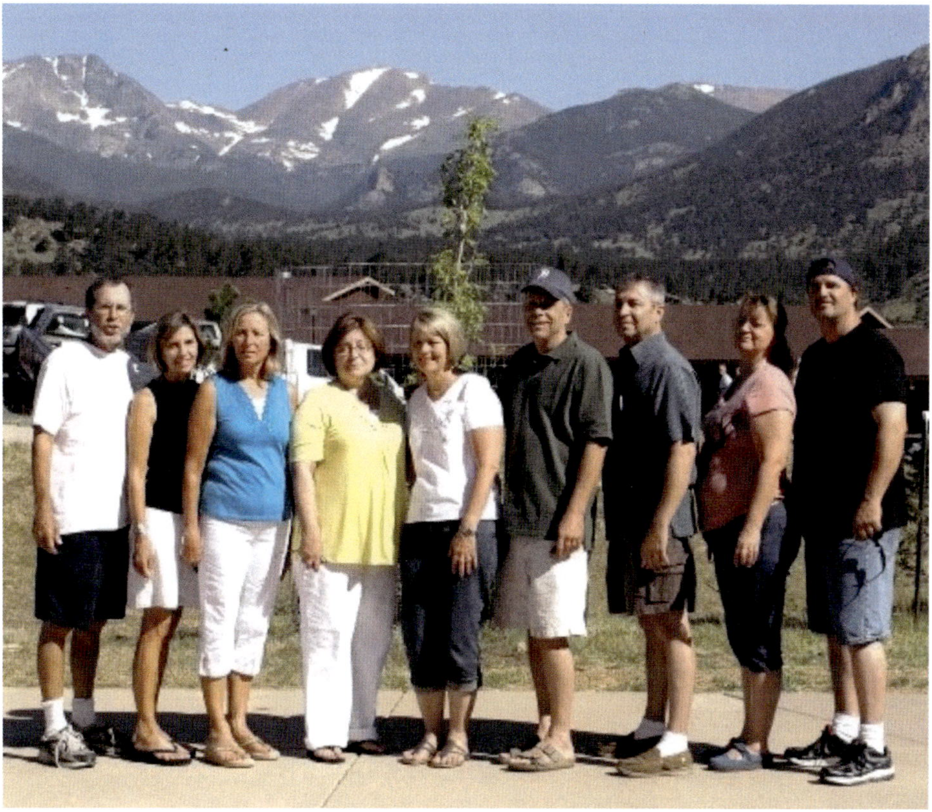

"THE BRITTLE RIDDLE"

by Jack Anderson

A short story based on true events.

"When life gives you lemons, make lemonade. When life gives you crates of lemons, stack them high enough to reach the apples you wanted in the first place and make apple pie. - This story is my feeble attempt to make American apple pie."

-Jack Anderson (Andy) #8

Copyright – all rights reserved.

All proceeds from the sale of this book go to: https://www.dnajustice.org/ . DNA Justice™ is a 501(c)(3) nonprofit dedicated to helping law enforcement agencies solve their most intractable cases while providing answers to families of victims. The DNA Justice database is built for volunteers to upload their DNA results exclusively for law enforcement comparison against profiles of perpetrators and unidentified human remains for identification purposes.

-The Andersons

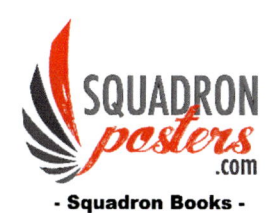

Made in the USA
Las Vegas, NV
15 February 2024